To Fall

FOR WINTER

KELSEY KINGSLEY

COPYRIGHT

Cover: Danny Manzella

Editor: Jessica Blaikie

For Danny—

My kind of crazy.

A LETTER FROM ME TO YOU

Dear Reader,

You might be new to me, you might be an old friend. Either way, hello! Glad to have you here with me in the next installment of the Kinney Brothers series.

So, I wanted to sit you down and give you a little look into who I am as a person. Now, before you roll your eyes and skip through this stupid little letter, let me just say … I promise I won't be long.

I'm not what you'd consider a conventional person.

I am tattooed. I am pierced. I wear combat boots. I collect skulls. I have only ever owned black cats. I live for Halloween. My favorite poet is Edgar Allen Poe, Stephen King was my first literary hero, and my favorite movie is *The Crow*. I love vampires and ravens and loud music and … you get the point.

But then … *Breakfast at Tiffany's* is one of the best movies I've ever seen, and I strongly believe we need more Audrey Hepburns in this world. I am absolutely *obsessed* with *Frasier* and *Outlander*. I have a soft spot for gentle love songs, and I really, really love a good romance novel.

Oh, and I also write romance novels. In case you weren't already aware.

Which, by the way, not many people expected me to do. Because people tend to judge by the cover, don't they? They take a look at someone, and they think they know everything there is to know by that first glance. They make their assumptions. They decide they know what's *right* with you, and what's *wrong*.

I wanted to break those rules with this book, by creating Ryan and Snow. People with a tough exterior, with all of the insecurities and deep thinking you'd expect from someone … *softer*. To maybe show another side to those unconventional people, to show that there is more to them beyond all that ink and metal.

There's love, there's pain, and maybe a touch of crazy. Not quite there.

But maybe that's all life is about. Finding your own flavor of insanity.

Maybe this book is yours.

Sincerely,
Kelsey

PROLOGUE
GOOD BROTHERS & CATS

I tried to convince myself it didn't matter to me. I tried so feckin' hard to tell myself that Cheryl kicking me out was the right thing. Because, well, she had said it herself—*I couldn't be domesticated.*

But who the hell was I kidding?

My chest hurt. My body hurt. My heart hurt.

Everything hurt.

The letter in my hand didn't help at all. Hanging from my fingers like a used, wilted tissue. Some stupid analogy about our relationship, about me, about every aspect of my feckin' life.

Patrick's truck pulled up to the curb and my older brother climbed out. He approached me slowly, as though I were about to lash out at him, but let's be honest. I didn't have the energy to *lash out*. Not after beating my fists against Cheryl's door until they were bruised. Not after dropping to my knees and begging her to just open the feckin' door and talk to me.

And nothing drained me more than calling my brother and admitting I needed help.

"Hey," Paddy said, stuffing his hands into his pockets. I glanced momentarily at his face, but there was sympathy there and I didn't want it.

I got to my feet, grabbing a few bags that Cheryl had so lovingly packed for me, and threw them into the bed of the truck. Not caring what was in them, not caring if I was breaking anything. I grabbed two more, tossed one in, and when something shattered from inside the bag, Patrick grabbed my arm before I could throw again.

"Ryan, let me do this, okay? Just get in the truck."

"I got it." My voice was graveled from all of my shouting earlier. It was a miracle the neighbors hadn't called the cops.

I attempted to pull my arm back to toss another bag in, but Patrick held strong and with a hard, angry stare at him, I dropped the thing to the ground. He picked it up and placed it in, and then pointed his finger at the cab.

"Ryan, just get in the goddamn truck, okay?"

My chest tightened, my throat restricted, and I turned to look at the house I had lived in for six months of my life. I hated that I felt the overwhelming urge to cry. I hated that, after everything, I was ready to run back up that walkway and beat my fists against the door until they were bleeding.

Patrick touched my arm. "Come on, Ryan," he said, talking to me the way he talked to his daughter in the middle of a tantrum. I was caught between appreciating it and wanting to punch him in the throat as I sighed and turned toward the truck.

I reached for the rusted handle on the door, and I remembered one important thing Cheryl hadn't tossed to the curb. My breath hitched in my throat, and I spun around to look at Patrick with wide-eyed panic.

"She has my feckin' cats," I somehow managed to croak around the blockade in my throat. One stupid tear broke free, sliding over my cheek and into my beard.

He came to me, gripping my shoulders in his hands. "Get in and don't move. I'll go get them, okay?"

I nodded and obeyed, opening the door and sliding into the cab as he walked up to the house with that authoritative gait he had learned from years on the force. I watched him knock, and although his voice didn't quite pass through the closed window, I heard him say something. Probably to tell her it was only him.

That she didn't have to be afraid, that it was safe. *Because it wasn't me.*

Sitting on the porch with three cat carriers at my feet, I listened to the murmurs of my parents and older brother coming from inside the house.

At least they weren't fighting. That was a good sign.

That's what I had expected when Patrick suggested we go to Mam and Da, to see if they could give me a place to stay. I expected a big fat *NO*, after everything I had put the two of them through. But they were speaking calmly in there, and that had to be a good sign, right?

The door opened and Da walked out onto the porch, the hinges creaking behind him. He sat next to me on the wicker couch and tilted his head toward the cigarette between my fingers.

"Would ya mind?" he asked, and without saying a word, I put it out in the planter to my right. With a sigh, Da pinched the space between his eyes. "I keep tellin' your mother we need to get somethin' if you're gonna keep up with that habit."

I shrugged apologetically. "I could quit if—"

He shook his head. "Don't quit on my account. Do that for yourself." He tipped his head back, looking out at the nighttime River Canyon sky. "There's a lot of things ya gotta want for yourself, Ryan."

"What does that mean?"

One hand gripped my shoulder. It was a small gesture, but my throat clenched with unexpected emotion. It had been years since I had allowed myself a conversation on the porch with my father, or either of my parents, for that matter. I was always on the move. Always doing something stupid. Always getting in trouble.

Why did it have to take getting my arse kicked to the curb to sit down with him?

Da shook his head. "Son … your mother and I have tried to figure ya out since ya were a wee lad. It's not even the tattoos or all these, y'know …" He pinched a piercing-free spot on my ear and tugged gently. "It's not that. We could deal with all that. But when you started gettin' into *all* that drinkin' and partyin', and y'know, those, ehm, instances with the drugs …"

He sighed heavily, and I remembered those moments: getting caught, getting arrested. I'd been reprimanded, and I had fought back, insisting that it wasn't *that bad* because it was *just weed*.

Why hadn't I taken anything more seriously?

"I know, Da," I mumbled, pushing a hand into my hair.

"We really hoped that, ehm …" He shifted uncomfortably beside me. Something told me he was about to bring *her* up, and he did. "Well, we thought that Cheryl would be good for ya. Seemed to work for a time, but …" His shoulders slumped, not exhuming the energy to shrug.

His hand touched my back. "So, what happened?"

"What *happened*?" I shot at him. He removed his hand, and I tried hard not to focus on the lack of touch. How empty it made me feel. "I'll tell ya what happened: *I* happened, that's what. She got me that feckin' job at the feckin' vet's. They said they needed a *groomer*, and what did they have me doin'? Cleanin' cages, because they didn't want me *dealin' with the public*."

His brows lowered. "They said that?"

"You bet your arse they said that, and when I said somethin' to Cheryl about it, all she said was, 'Well, what do ya expect, Ryan? Look at you.'" I swallowed twice before I could encourage myself to push forward. "Anyway, they finally fired me yesterday."

"She kicked ya out because ya got fired?"

I gave him a half-hearted shrug. "I think it was a combination of that, and gettin' drunk and breaking a couple things on my way into the house last night."

I sighed and slumped into the couch, resting my head against the hard wicker back. "I tried to find another job today, came up empty, and when I got back home, there was a note on the door and my shite was on the lawn." I swept my hand in a gesture toward the cat carriers at my feet. "Except the cats. Paddy had to get them."

"Ya have a good brother," Da said.

I hung my head and nodded. I really did—two of them: Patrick and Sean. Hell, my entire family was good. Supportive. Accepting. They had saved me from a lot of shite in the past—jail, trouble, booze, drugs, ex-girlfriends.

Maybe they could save me from myself.

Pushing both hands through my hair and holding them around the back of my throbbing skull, I planted my elbows on my knees.

Taking my pride and setting it aside, I found the courage to say, "Da, I need help."

Da's hand was against my back again. "You can't change for someone else, son. You have to want it for—"

"It's not for *her*," I spat, staring at my boots and the three cat carriers.

I needed it for me. I needed it if I was ever going to be good enough for someone *like her*. I needed it before I was too lost in my own mess, and God knows I couldn't clean it up myself.

Da nodded, patting my back.

"Okay," he said. "Okay."

ଈ

And for two years, I was convinced I was cured. Until Snow came to town.

CHAPTER ONE
CIGARETTES & SNOW

Snow came to River Canyon on the first day of winter.

Ha. It's only hit me, just now, how absolutely feckin' absurd that sounds. And actually, now that I think of it, *absurd* is the perfect word to describe it all.

She walked into the clinic—the River Canyon Animal Clinic—completely by accident, thinking our door was the entrance to Canvas & Ink, or so I thought at the time. I looked up from the reception desk, disturbed from a rousing game of Solitaire and time with the sketchbook in my lap, and immediately, that didn't matter, because …

Well … Holy Hell.

She had on this loose-fitting black sweater, tight black jeans, and these combat boots that I would've begged to have my arse kicked with. The whole outfit matched her long hair and smudged eye makeup: jet black.

Everything was black, except for her lips. Her lips were full and pink, and they looked feckin' soft. A gothic princess with that one hint of femininity.

I wanted her.

Instant attraction, that's exactly what it was. An immediate surge of blood flow from my brain straight down to my crotch and thank the baby Christ for desks.

Before I could say anything, she had strolled in with those boots, bouncing their rubber soles against the bleached linoleum. She took a quick look around, then settled her black-rimmed eyes on me, and laughed.

Immediately my eyebrows shot upward, and then furrowed. Anxious paranoia crept up from the neck of my scrubs, spreading a radiant heat over my face, and I stupidly wondered if she had actually seen my erection through the desk.

"What's so—"

Her hand covered her mouth, her muffled giggles persisted. "This *definitely* isn't the tattoo shop."

And yeah, I guess that could explain the laughter. So, I shook my head, loosened my brow, and relaxed a little. "Nope, sorry to disappoint, but hey, if you need dewormin', you've come to the right place."

She looked me over with a slight tilt of her head and stepped forward slowly; walking in this way that told me she held the reins. She was looking me over with a cocktail of lust and assertiveness, and when she reached the desk, I noticed just how crystal blue her eyes were. The woman could have sucked the soul from the Devil himself with eyes like that, and it was all I could do to not offer my body up for sacrifice.

"I've never seen a male secretary before."

The comment was so blunt it startled me, and I laughed. "Well, I'm also the resident groomer."

One side of her pretty mouth quirked, pulling it into this little half-smile. Her pierced nose wrinkled just a little. "Yeah, okay, but I'm more intrigued by the secretary part. Is this town really so small that you can't hire anybody else?"

I met her eye with my own lopsided smile, challenging her. "Why bother slashin' my paycheck if I can manage to do both?"

She nodded, and pursed those lips, putting them on display. "I suppose you make a compelling argument," she said, but then she tilted her head, her questioning eyes lingering just a little too long.

"What?" I asked, feeling too on the spot for my liking.

She smiled with just the slightest shake of her head. "Nothing. It's just … Well, I just wouldn't have expected a guy like you to be sitting behind a desk … taking orders."

I knew from the moment she walked in that she would be trouble, and that comment was all the clarification I needed.

"And what would you know about a guy like me?"

"Well … I know from looking at you, and from that motorcycle sitting outside, that you're a badass. I know from the way you're looking at me that you don't like someone else having the upper hand. But … then again, maybe you *like* letting someone else take control." I watched her mouth form that word: *control*. Watched it pass through her puckered lips.

God, why did they look so feckin' soft?

"Maybe I do," I quipped, and immediately wondered why the hell I had to reply at all.

"Hmm …" She took a step backward, watching me with her ethereal eyes and coy smile before turning to venture around the room. She strolled, taking in the posters of cats and dogs, pictures of my boss and I. She pointed to a framed photo of the clinic from when I first started working, two years ago.

She turned to me. "This is you."

I nodded. "Yep."

"And this studious looking fellow is your boss?" She tapped the glass with one black fingernail.

"Business partner," I falsely corrected, raising my level on the food chain just a bit. Even if it *was* total BS.

Her eyes were lie detectors, and she smiled as though she were about to chastise me, but her eyes glinted with the slightest touch of sympathy. "*His* name is on the door though, unless *you're* Doctor Matthew Sinclair."

"No, I'm not," I replied, focusing on that sympathetic flicker that kept passing over her gaze. It left me shaken, and I shifted in my seat.

"I know," she chided, pointing at the picture. "You're Ryan, says so right here. Ryan Kinney."

Well, so much for introductions.

I shrugged. "We run the place together."

"Oh, I doubt that, but even if you *are* telling the truth, you're replaceable, Mr. Secretary; he's not."

My jaw clenched, and I dropped my gaze back to the game of Solitaire on the screen, clicking the mouse to appear busy. Obviously, I had some super important secretarial work to tend to. You know, appointments to book, vaccines to schedule. Strange, nosy women to ignore. Nosy women with soft looking lips.

Christ, she had gotten under my skin, and I had known her for all of three minutes.

And why is this turning me on so much?

"Hey, just calling it like I see it," she said, casually lifting one shoulder in a half-shrug. Her sweater fell down an inch, revealing the tattooed lines of tree branches.

"Canvas & Ink is next door," I replied with a hard edge to my voice, reminding her of what she was doing here in the first place. Before she disrupted my day of important card games and sketchbooks.

"I'm sorry. I didn't mean to upset you. My mouth gets carried away sometimes," she said, shrugging. The sweater drooped a little more, and I could see more of those branches.

My curiosity was piqued, but my nonchalance remained intact. "It's fine," I grunted, clicking around the screen as my mind wondered what else her mouth enjoyed doing.

As I worked to ignore her, my hand rounded to the back of my neck to relieve an itch.

She took a couple steps back toward the desk. "What's that?"

"What's what?" I grumbled indifferently.

"On your wrist?"

The arm of my shirt had slid upward, revealing just a peek of the sleeve inked to my skin.

"Ehm, tattoos?"

"Can I see?" Her eyes sparkled with excited intrigue, and because she had asked, I rolled my shirt sleeve to my elbow. "Impressive." She bit her pretty bottom lip and nodded her approval, as though I needed it, and for some reason, I felt that I did. "What about the other arm?" And because she had asked, I rolled the other shirt sleeve up too. Again, she nodded, before rolling the sleeves of her sweater up, as far as they would allow. A mural of black and white painted both arms, an eye-catching contrast to her snow-white skin.

"Impressive," I said, mimicking, but I was also honest. In fact, I was *thoroughly* impressed, and even more turned on. If I was hard before, I was now made of stone. So … I decided to pry. "What else do you have?"

Her hands gripped the edge of the desk, and she leaned forward a bit. The neckline of her sweater dipped lower, flashing the rounded tops of tattooed breasts. "I'll show you mine, if you show me yours," and she grinned in that coy little way.

At that, all residual effects of her demeaning my job flew out the window, and I was ready to bend her over my desk right then and there. My groin throbbed with a lustful desperation that told me it had been too long since I had gotten laid, and that if she didn't get out of there soon, I was going to give my boss a very good reason to replace me.

She smiled, as though she were considering something, and then she nodded. "I like you."

And what in the hell was I supposed to say to that? I mean, Christ, I had been with my fair share of women. *Too* many women, some would say. But, of all the women I had been with, or even known, none of them had ever possessed this remarkable ability to honestly speak their mind without being coaxed.

"Do you like me?" she asked, her eyes flashing just the faintest hint of hope.

"I don't even know you," I said with a laugh that floated somewhere between a giggle and a chuckle.

What the feck was that? The woman had made me giggle. Have I *ever* giggled before in my life?

Her crystalline eyes flashed with confident delight. "Come on Ryan. It's not a hard question. You can know in a few seconds if you *like* someone or not. It's not a freakin' marriage proposal." She bit that lip again—hopeful, coy, and so feckin' sexy.

That much was true. It wasn't a proposal, and I actually knew I liked her the moment she walked through that door. All of that black and those soft pink lips, and so I shrugged. "Yeah, sure. I like ya."

"Good," she said, satisfied, and turned on her heel. "I'll see you around, Mr. Secretary."

֍

Later that night, as I I left through the front door, the cool winter air whipped against my forehead and bit my nose. I squinted my eyes to ward off the sting, and as I locked the door behind me, I fantasized about the cigarette I was going to have before heading to my apartment in my grandmother's basement.

I braced myself against the gust of wind, turned in the direction of my bike, and stopped dead in my tracks.

My motorcycle waited for me at the curb, the chrome glinting under the picturesque lamppost, and … there she was. Sitting on my bike, like she already held some claim over it.

Over me?

I noticed her raven hair immediately, gleaming under the streetlamps. Her hands were wrapped inside the long sleeves of her black sweater, while her legs bounced rapidly against the sidewalk. From the looks of her, I would have guessed she was freezing. Her eyes were shut, her cheeks were wind-bitten red, and her lips had turned a deeper shade of pink. But she was also happy. A serene smile stretched from ear-to-ear, and it was in that moment that I found her not only intriguing and sexy as hell, but I knew that I had done it again.

I was attracted to yet another woman who wasn't *quite there.*

I never liked to call it crazy, and I never liked to call it unstable, because what would that make me? But it was something, and I was attracted to it—*it* was attracted to me. And together, we made a mess. There was no balance. No boundaries to keep our out-of-control personalities contained.

And this woman and me? There was no doubt in my mind that we would make a mess.

But dammit, I couldn't keep myself from getting dirty.

"Hey. That's my bike." I walked toward her, keeping my gait steady, though my brain willed my feet to run far, far away.

"I know." Her eyes met mine, she smiled, and I hunkered further into my scarf, reaching into my pocket for my smokes.

She simply crossed one leg over the other, solidifying her resilience to move. I sniffed a chuckle, hidden by the wind. I could have moved her myself. I could have wrapped one arm around that tiny waist and hauled her right off without breaking a sweat. But I just couldn't stop my itching curiosity, and I had to know what kept that arse sitting on the seat of my bike.

Her eyes flickered with temptation at the sight of the cigarettes, her tongue darting between her lips, and I held the open carton out to her. Without speaking a word, she plucked one, eyed it critically, then slid it back in and selected another.

I raised my pierced brow. "What's wrong with this one?" I pulled her reject from the pack, placed it between my teeth, and stuffed the smokes back in my pocket.

She shrugged, swinging her foot around in small circles. "This one looked better. You have a light?"

"Nah, I thought I'd stand here and pretend to smoke while I freeze my balls off," I grumbled through clenched teeth, my cigarette dancing as I spoke, and I grabbed my lighter. Flipping it open, I lit mine, and held the light out to her. She leaned into it, cupped her fingerless-gloved hand around the dancing flame, and set her cigarette alight.

We enjoyed our cigarettes together, and while we smoked, I eyed her through my play of indifference. Standing over her, sending smoke curling above her head, I wondered what her deal was. But instead of asking, I took note once again of her rosy cheeks and wind-stung nose.

"Aren't you cold?"

"No, I love the winter."

"So do I, but loving winter doesn't mean you can't freeze to death. You should have a coat on. It's freezin' out here."

She closed her eyes as she took a long drag and held the smoke in her lungs before sending it dancing into the air. Then she opened her eyes again, stabbing me with the stained-glass icicles in her irises.

"I'm okay, but it's sweet that you care," she said to me, bouncing her one boot against the sidewalk, the other dangling in the air. "You know, I was actually waiting out here for you."

"Oh, yeah?" I smiled, intrigued. "Why didn't ya just come inside, then?"

"Where are you from?" she asked, changing the topic entirely.

My arms spread out wide, cigarette dangling between my lips. "You're lookin' at it."

She shook her head, her mouth spreading into a little smile. "That accent is *definitely* not from around here. It's weird."

I laughed. "Weird, huh?"

Her eyes narrowed a bit in concentration, smoke framed her face and faded with the wind. "Yeah, *weird*. Like when people mate a couple random fruits together and call it something stupid, like a *tangelo* or *grapple* or some shit like that, and they label it *Designer*, when really, it's just a science experiment that happened to work out really well." She sucked in a long drag, cheeks hollowing. She dropped her hand, exhaled. Smoke spiraled in the air. She let loose a little amused smile. "You're … *Not Quite American*. That's your designer label."

"I have absolutely no idea what you're talkin' about," I said with a low chuckle, clenching the cigarette between my teeth.

"See, weird like that … *Talkin'*," she mocked playfully. "A word gets thrown in there, and you're suddenly Scottish."

"Hey," I pointed at her. "I'm definitely *not* Scottish."

"You have something against Scottish people?"

"Not at all." I took a drag and released. "Just don't want to be labelled somethin' I'm not."

"Then," she said, pointing her toe in my direction, "I ask again, where are you from?"

"Born in Ireland, moved here as a baby, and was raised by a wild pack of Irish people." I rolled my eyes up to the billowing cloud of smoke that wafted from my mouth and nostrils, watched it for all of two seconds, before the fresh winter chill could rob it of life and it disappeared.

I expected more questions, because there usually were. Women loved the accent, as slight as it might have been more often than not, and they always loved to know more. About my family, my upbringing, the "homeland." Or, better yet, they liked to throw words at me, to demand I say them with the learned, dormant brogue that would most likely land me a night between their legs.

It was my secret weapon; always getting me into trouble.

But this woman? Nah, she wasn't like the rest. I already knew that, but she was about to make that point exceptionally clear.

"So ..." She shifted slightly, rolling her soft-looking, pink lips between her teeth. "What are you doing tonight?"

"What am *I* doing tonight?"

"Is there someone else here I'm not aware of?" she teased with a quirk of a brow.

I snorted, scratching the back of my neck. "Just makin' sure I heard you right. Why? Did you wanna, ehm ..." I didn't know what to say. Offer to take her to the Ol' Tavern for a drink? I didn't drink. Maybe suggest checking out the William Fuller statue? Too touristy for my tastes.

She had ideas of her own, though. "I'd actually like to have sex with you tonight."

She looked up at me expectantly, and with the cigarette between my fingers, I took a long drag, staring down at her through relaxed hooded eyes that I hoped weren't giving away the serious freak-out happening inside my head.

But *Christ*, that was something new.

In all my years of partying and having women toss themselves at me, I couldn't think of a time when one of them had just come up to me and so plainly said exactly what they wanted. Sure, I knew my cock had been on their minds when they hung from my arm or wrapped themselves around my neck. I knew sex was ultimately what they were after, but in some desperate need to behave as the little ladies their mamas had raised them to be, they never said it. Not like that. Not sober. Not without even batting an eye. No, they needed it to be my idea—my *fault*, if it went badly, if it was awkward.

Hell, I almost thought this woman was joking. A twisted deadpan line that I wasn't finding particularly funny. I waited for a laugh, the telltale glimmer of amusement, but you know what I saw? Cold, icy eyes. They frisked my bundled-up body, checking for signs of my own arousal. And she saw it, and her eyes twinkled with anticipation.

"So, you're serious?" My voice was tight, strangled. I had held the smoke in too long, and I coughed.

"Nobody's ever propositioned you for sex before?" she asked, and there was that lip bite again. "I somehow doubt that."

My cheeks puffed around a sigh. I chuckled awkwardly. "Ehm, well, they usually want me to at least buy 'em a drink first."

"But if all you want is to sleep with someone, why go through all that? Why not just go straight to the good stuff?"

I laughed again. Less awkward, more surprise. "Because it's the right thing to do?"

"According to who though?"

She tipped her head to one side. Her long black hair slid off her shoulder, and the streetlamps illuminated the white skin of her neck, peeking out through the tangle of tattooed tree branches. They came around from the back, and I wanted to see what they were attached to. I wanted to sink my teeth into them, trace them with my tongue.

I closed my eyes, pinching the bridge of my nose, because I didn't have an answer to her question. "All I know is, women typically prefer it when men at least make a bit of an effort before sleepin' with 'em."

"What if I don't want effort though? What if I just want to get laid?"

"I don't do one-night stands."

She raised a disbelieving eyebrow, crystal-blue eyes staring right through me. "Come on Ryan, you don't know me … there's really no reason to lie."

"And you know *me*?" I asked laughing, and scratched the back of my head, cigarette pinched between my fingers. I was officially perplexed by that tiny woman with the frozen eyes.

She slowly licked her lips, considering her next words while teasing me. "Okay, look … What is the first thing you want to do when you see an attractive woman? Do you want to bring her flowers, take her out to dinner, make her fall in love with you, and *then* have sex?"

I gripped my neck. When had I started sweating? "I, ehm—"

"No," she cut me off with the raising of one finger, "because you want to know her in a carnal way, because you're an animal before you're human, and animals fuck, Ryan. You want to make her yours, mark your territory, make sure nobody else gets to her first, and only *then* do you get to know her."

"Jesus feckin' Christ." I cleared my throat, shaking my head and pushing my hands back through my hair.

She chuckled a little under her breath. "Ireland, life is too short to have shitty sex. What happens if we fall in love, and then find out the sex is horrible? Then what?"

She had nicknamed me, and to top it off, she had mentioned being in love, as though she expected that to be a real possibility in our future. She did all of this, brought me to a personal level, and I didn't even know her name.

Red flags galore.

"Then, we're in love, and we have shitty sex," I offered weakly.

"Spoken like a guy who's never been in love with a woman who knew what she was doing."

She threw the butt of her cigarette to the sidewalk, and got off the bike, further proving how much smaller than me she really was. I could've taken that tiny woman and shoved her in my pocket, if I wanted to. But instead, I just watched as she stomped the cigarette remains into the pavement, and she looked up at me.

"Come on Ryan. You're really gonna tell me you haven't wanted to sleep with me since I walked through that door?" She confidently reached two little fingers forward, hooked them into the belt loops on my jeans, and pulled herself forward. Her body pressed against mine, and I didn't move, if only for the sake of keeping her from freezing to death. But I didn't touch her. Didn't react. Didn't even feckin' breathe.

If I wasn't wearing my leather jacket and a thick sweatshirt underneath, I knew I would have felt the mounds of her breasts pressed against my stomach.

The thought of her tits, the thought of what they might look like outside of that sweater, the thought of what she might look like on the brink of orgasmic bliss at the mercy of my hands, or dick, or mouth, or hell … all three. *This* is what had me standing there on the sidewalk, hard as steel, and considering the unexpected offer laid at my feet.

I knew it was an arsehole move to even consider it, and I knew there was a pretty good chance I would later kick myself had I gone through with it. Because it had been two whole years since I had promised to turn over a new leaf, and the last thing I wanted to do was break my streak of good behavior.

But … I was also a man. And I was intrigued by this enigma of a woman who was confident and capable of being honest, who knew exactly what she wanted and wasn't afraid to say it.

"What's your name?" I asked, almost breathless in a voice gruff with carnal intent.

She smiled smugly. Soft, pink lips tilted upward; the confident smile twitching at the corners.

She knew she had me.

"Snow."

My lips twitched with amusement. "Snow? Really?"

"Yes."

"Okay then." I dropped my forgotten cigarette to the ground, crushing it underneath my boot, and walked toward my bike. "Get on."

And that was how I met Snow.

CHAPTER TWO
HONESTY & DISAPPOINTMENTS

When I was seventeen, my older brother Patrick had a momentary lapse of judgment with a girl he couldn't stand, and as luck would have it, he had gotten the chick pregnant.

The night he was told about the pregnancy, he came home and with his head in his hands, he gave our parents the *wonderful* news. I walked in on that cheerful little conversation, coming in from a night of partying with my friends. I had looked at him—ghost-white and panicked. Then, I looked at my parents—fuming and also panicked. The three of them had acted for a time as though they were the only ones being affected by it all, but in truth, it was a defining moment in all of our lives.

For our parents, it was the shock of being handed their Grandparent Card before they felt they were ready. It was the reality that their oldest son, their first baby, was having a baby of his own and embarking on a journey of life that would take him places they weren't permitted.

For Patrick, it was the rusty—albeit temporary—nail in the coffin that held his relationship with his childhood sweetheart. It was the consequence to trump all others. And, well, I also like to think it was one of the best things to ever happen to him, because I know now that he sees his daughter as anything but a mistake.

For my twin brother Sean, it was the encouragement he needed to continue being the *perfect son*. It was the pressure to get good grades, keep his head above water, and although he never said it, it stressed the shite out of him. I could see it in the lines that had formed between his brows.

As for me? *Well …*

On that night, after sneaking up to the bedroom I still shared with Sean, all I can remember thinking was, "Well, nothing I do can ever be as disappointing as this. That guy has set the bar, and I will never see myself over it." And that would have been fine, except that, for me, it wasn't a warning—it became a dare, and I tested it a little too much. I managed to pass over that bar by the time I was twenty, and I just kept on climbing.

And it wasn't that I was a bad guy, keep in mind. I just couldn't seem to help myself. I just found trouble, or maybe it found me. Who the hell knows.

Still, by some miracle, I had never knocked a girl up.

Maybe things would have been better if I had.

And this was what I thought about while Snow and I did the cliché bullshite of having a smoke after sex.

But you know, she had been right.

About the sex, I mean.

I had never been in love with a woman who knew what she was doing. Not like being with her. No, she had been something else.

Her mouth tasted of coffee and menthol; the familiar addictions tantalizing my own senses. Her skin was chilled to the touch, no matter the temperature of the room, but inside, she enveloped me in a comfortable, snug warmth. The scent of the crisp outdoors and a woodsy perfume clung to her skin and hair, reminding me instantly of fireplaces and frosty nights.

And for that solid hour of getting to know her in the rawest of ways, it dawned on me that she was the embodiment of winter, and just as unpredictable. One moment, she was mild and sweet, biting her bottom lip in that coy little way that drove me crazy. Then the next, she was controlling my every move, telling me exactly what she wanted and where. She didn't play guessing games, she didn't leave me fumbling or questioning. She guided my hands and my mouth; using my body for her personal benefit. So many other girls might have been a giggling bundle of shyness, saying the dirty words that came out of her mouth, but not Snow.

It was a rare, fine thing that I relished and devoured for a solid hour. Because Christ, how could I have possibly lasted longer than two years before doing something stupid, reckless, and *good* like this?

"What are you thinking about?" She broke the silence, tapping one of her fingers against my chest, and I looked down at her. Her eyes met mine with a little smile. "And please, don't say some lame shit, like how beautiful I am. Be honest."

My mouth twisted into an amused smirk. "What if that *is* what I'm thinkin'?"

"Because you're not even looking at me, Ireland," she retorted with her own smirk and a light giggle. She tapped my chest again. "Come on. Tell me, and remember—be honest."

Narrowing my eyes, I took a moment to ponder the question, to find my answer, and finally said, "I'm thinkin' that—"

"Nope, you hesitated. Try again."

My brow furrowed, shifting my jaw from side to side. "Ehm, well …"

"Knock it off Ireland. Come on, tell me *exactly* what you're thinking. One, two, three … *Go.*"

On the spot, I blurted it out: "I'm such a feckin' disappointment."

She raised herself up on an elbow, looking at me with her icicle eyes. "Why do you say that?"

I bit my lower lip, chewing before shoving the cigarette back in my mouth. I diverted my eyes from hers, letting the smoke dangle between my teeth. I smoothed a wrinkle out on the bed for no particular reason other than it was something to do. Something other than looking at her, and the eyes that threatened to freeze me to death.

"You have to answer the question," she said, her voice soft.

"Why?"

"Because that's all part of our deal."

"*Our deal?*" I laughed, unsuccessfully fighting the smile that tugged at my lips. "I think that was all you, babe."

"Yeah, well," she said, "we didn't have shitty sex, so *now*, I want to know more about you."

Finally, I looked back at her, plucking the cigarette from my teeth. "You could ask my favorite color, or if I like walkin' barefoot in the sand."

"Oh, because *that's* important," she laughed, shaking her head with an eye roll. "No, come on. Just answer the question. It's not that difficult. You have nothing to lose by telling me."

She had a point there.

"Fine." I sighed and grabbed for the ashtray on the night stand, stamping my smoke into it. "I've done a lot of stupid shite throughout my life, and I asked my parents for help a couple years ago. I told them I was ready to grow up, and they must've been so feckin' *thrilled* to hear me say that, because they jumped at the opportunity to sort me out, as long as I promised to not screw it up again."

"What kind of stupid *shite*?" she asked, her voice full of intrigue. Her mockery of my accent and learned language didn't irritate me the way it usually did.

Another red flag, waving in the winter wind. Another red flag, going ignored.

"Ah, well, let's see … I was arrested twice—"

"Ooh, a man with a record." She grinned at me, rubbing her hands together. "I *knew* you were a bad boy."

I laughed. "Oh, yeah, it's *real* impressive," I said with an eye roll, "especially when one of those times, it was my brother puttin' the cuffs on. *That* was a *whole* lot of fun."

She winced. "Wow, that's an awkward family dinner waiting to happen."

I pursed my lips and nodded at the ceiling. "Might've been, if I hadn't already been arrested once and slapped on the wrist countless times. Ya know, it just became somethin' they expected from me, I guess." I shrugged. "Anyway, then there were the hospital visits …"

"Do I want to know?"

"Once I broke my leg jumpin' off a roof."

She laughed. "Why the hell would you do that?"

"Because I was high, and my friend told me to do it."

"Good reason." I heard the eye-roll in her sarcastic tone, and I couldn't say that I blamed her. It was a dumb thing only a dumb kid would do, and it was even dumber still that I hadn't been a kid at all. I had been twenty-three.

I decided to leave out the admission that the other hospital visit had come to pass because an ex-girlfriend decided to stab me. I figured that could be a story for another day, or you know … Maybe never.

"Anyway," I said in a tired, heavy voice, "I've made a lot of dumb choices, borrowed a lot of money for stupid things, got fired from a lot of jobs, and had a handful of terrible ex-girlfriends. So, yeah, I was kind of a wreck, and my parents had to step in and clean shite up."

"And now, you think that by sleeping with me, you went back on your promise?" I hesitated, and she shook her head. "Stop stalling," she scolded lightly, tugging gently at my beard.

And I did. "Yeah."

I expected her to flip out, to jump from the bed, collect her clothes and storm out. To make things really awkward when I saw her again in that tiny town. It's what another woman would have done, after being told they were the reason you were feeling like an absolute piece of shite for doing what you had just done.

But, not Snow. She wasn't one to be predictable or act like any other woman.

She smiled, satisfied, and settled her head against my chest. "I like you a lot, Ireland."

"Because I'm a disappointment?"

"No." I felt her lips against my chest, right over my heart. "I like you, because you're loyal."

She raised her hand to my mouth, placing her cigarette between my lips. I found myself smiling, treating myself to the last drag of a smoke that had been touched by her pretty mouth, and I put it out in the ashtray.

"Get me something to drink," she demanded sweetly and patted my bearded cheek.

I laughed as she rolled off to the side of the bed. She laid flat on her back, raising her arms above her head, propping one knee up, and Christ. I couldn't stop looking at her.

Slender and small with a delicate bone structure—she reminded me of a bird in that way. Her skin was glowing white and ink black, the contrast startling and breathtaking. With the smudged black makeup, the black hair, the black painted on her finger and toe nails, I thought she looked like a black-and-white movie star. Old fashioned beauty with the modern enhancements of intricately detailed tattoos.

I was so screwed.

I swallowed, rolling up from the bed. "So, what would ya like?"

"Well, what do you have?"

"Water. Coffee. That's about it."

She raised an eyebrow, twirling a strand of her dark hair flirtatiously around a finger. The rise and fall of her breasts hypnotized me, the jewelry in her nipples twinkling in the light.

Christ almighty. I swallowed, unable to take my eyes off of the gemmed barbells.

"No alcohol?" she asked, ripping me from my magpie impersonation.

And, ladies and gents, I had stumbled on the deal breaker. "Nah, I don't drink anymore."

"You are the shittiest Irishman ever," she laughed, tipping her head back and grinning at the ceiling as though it were the funniest thing she had ever heard. "Is that your way of rebelling against the stereotype or something?"

"Or something," I growled out, my eyes wandering the length of her body. From the downward slope below her ribcage, to her two-times bejeweled navel, to that tiny bit of silver metal between her legs.

My eyes narrowed, my fists balled, my mouth salivated, and my breath hitched. Every part of my body fought, completely stuck between wanting to pounce on her again and kicking her out for poking fun at my decisions to keep a level head.

She raised her other leg, crossing it over her propped-up knee. The dainty foot with its black-polished nails danced in the air, and she smiled. "Guess what?"

"Hmm?" I grunted, leaning against the doorframe.

"I don't drink anymore either."

She was full of surprises. So unpredictable.

"Well, that settles it," I said with a spreading grin. "I'm buyin' ya dinner."

Snow smiled, pulling herself into a seated position. Her arms crossed over her legs, making her a tangle of tattooed limbs, and I knew there was no way I was going to let her leave before getting lost in her again.

"See, Ireland?"

"Hmm?" I asked with my sheepish smile, too busy staring to form any intelligible words.

"Sex first." She sighed. "Best way to get to know someone."

CHAPTER THREE
LITTLE DOGS & TEAMWORK

S now had moved into the apartment over Mrs. Montgomery the Church Lady's garage. With nothing other than what could fit into her little orange VW Beetle, her belongings were minimal. She didn't have much in the way of tables or chairs, and so she insisted we have dinner at my place.

"And eating out isn't an option, unless we're talking about your mouth on my ..." she said when she stopped by the clinic earlier the next day, a mischievous smile playing at her lips and pointer fingers aimed downward.

I choked on my coffee.

"What?" she smirked, not remotely embarrassed in the room full of two- and four-legged clients.

"I'd be grateful if ya didn't get me fired," I said after composing myself, surveying the room for onlookers while blotting at the spilled coffee on my shirt.

"Oh, excuse me, Mr. Secretary. I should've realized this town was full of sexless prudes," she teased with a theatrical roll of her eyes. "Tell me, where do the babies come from around here? Stork? Cabbage Patch?"

It was in that moment that Mayor Connie Fischer bounded through the door with her toy poodle clutched firmly in her arms. "Ryan!"

I glared at Snow, warning her with my eyes to keep her mouth shut, before addressing Connie. "Yeah Connie, what's up?"

"I need you to work your magic," she said urgently.

Snow crossed her arms and raised a mischievous eyebrow. "What does *this* woman know about your *magic*, Ryan?"

Connie took a hard look at Snow, the two women sizing each other up as though they really were fighting over me, and I scrubbed a hand over my face. "Mayor, this is Snow, the new tattoo artist."

"Hmm. I heard you were coming." Connie narrowed her eyes with blatant scrutiny at Snow, taking in her pitch-black hair and makeup, the tattoos on her hands, the piercings in her lip and nose. "No surprise you've already been acquainted with our Ryan."

Snow turned to wink at me. "Oh, we've been acquainted, all right."

I wanted to laugh, but I bit back my chuckle and scowled at her before turning back to Connie, reaching open hands across the desk. "Consider my magic worked. What are we doin' with him? What color ribbons?"

"Oh, the usual teddy bear cut. And the ribbons, hmm … Something Christ-like."

Connie pursed her lips and nodded with satisfaction at her choice as she placed the squirming little dog in my hands. I pulled him into my body and scratched him behind the ears. He looked up to me with pleading eyes, and I shot him a look that I hoped said, *"Sorry, pal. Nothin' I can do about the owner God graced ya with."*

"*Christ*-like?" Snow asked, shooting the Mayor a puzzled look, and when she didn't get any answers, she raised her eyebrows at me.

"Baxter plays Baby Jesus in the live-action Nativity scene every year," I supplied, and Connie scoffed.

"I asked Patrick and Kinsey if I could use Erin, because Lord knows that baby would make an excellent Christ, but *no*," she said with a scowl and a shake of her head. "I swear, everything I do for the people in this town … You would think it'd be nothing to let me borrow a baby for a night."

Snow bit her lip to suppress her laughter, her cheeks pinking just a bit under the fluorescent glow of the lights.

"Kinsey *is* stubborn." I nodded with agreement, my voice quivering on my own quelled chuckle.

"I even offered to let them play Mary and Joseph! Do you know what an *honor* that is? What more could they possibly want from me?"

"Couldn't say, Mayor." I shook my head

"You know … Ryan …"

Here we go. "Yeah?"

"He *is* your brother. Maybe you could—"

Yeah, not going there. "Y'know, Connie, I should probably get to work on this little guy," I said, cutting her off. "I mean, you want him to be ready before rehearsal, right?"

"Yes! Yes, of course. Remember, Ryan: *Christ-like.*" She flashed me the old Jazz Hands, and Snow had to turn around, pretending to stare at a poster of a Jack Russell while she squeezed her blackened lids shut, biting her tongue.

"You got it." I flashed her my best grin, and she bound out of the clinic.

When the door was closed, Snow lost her battle with the giggles and she covered her mouth with both hands. I chuckled along, but mostly I watched the tears collect in the corners of her eyes, wishing I had met this version of her *before* the version intent on sleeping with me. This playful version with her hair pulled back into a sleek ponytail, her lips looking particularly soft and kissable.

"Wow," she said breathlessly when the last of the giggles subsided.

I smiled. "And now you've met the Mayor."

"I already knew she was a nut. When I first got here, some little old lady mentioned that the Mayor banned everybody from parking on the street," Snow explained, her eyes twinkling with the warning of another giggle fit.

I grinned, leaning back in my seat with Baxter making himself at home in my lap. "Ah, right … The old *No Parked Vehicles Allowed on the Street* rule …"

She pursed her lips. "Wait a minute … If nobody can park on the street, how the hell do *you* get away with it?"

I shrugged with my hands, tipping my head against the back of the chair. "Must've worked my magic."

Her eyes widened, and her hands went straight to her hips as she leaned closer to my ear. "Oh my God, you've actually *slept* with that woman?"

The sincerity in her eyes was intense, and I almost thought I caught the faintest glint of jealousy in there.

I chuckled and shook my head. "Hell no."

Snow rolled her eyes playfully, standing up and crossing her arms. "Whatever you say, Mr. *I'm the Only One Allowed to Park on the Street*."

My laugh was impossible to keep contained. "Trust me, she's not my type. They were discussing the parking situation at a town board meeting, and I mentioned that I thought it'd be inconsiderate to other town residents if I were takin' up a whole parking space just for the bike," I said, one corner of my mouth upturning into a lopsided smile. And then I gestured for her to come closer, and when her ear was almost touching my lips, I whispered, "But really, I just didn't wanna have to make the walk from the parkin' lot all the way over here."

Snow giggled, and then harrumphed. "Well, maybe *I'd* like to reap those benefits as your, um, *friend*."

I shrugged, ignoring the very loud, very hard pitter-patter of my heart. "I'll drive ya to work, if you'd like."

"Good," she said, triumphant and smiling. And then, she reached over to pet Baxter. "So, Mr. Secretary, my lunch break is almost over, and we still haven't decided on dinner."

"You're really opposed to goin' somewhere?" I asked, reviving the original conversation.

"Yep."

"And why's that?" I asked, crossing my arms. "You don't wanna be seen with me?"

She twisted her lips into an amused little smirk. "Oh no, Ireland. I'd be happy to parade you around town, or anywhere. But as our first dinner together, it should be intimate; not surrounded by a restaurant full of nosy eavesdroppers who would just *love* to stare at the *town freaks.*"

Even in our bland little town, people knew better than to stare at me. My appearance didn't faze them—the ink, the piercings now went unnoticed, and since rolling into town, nobody had treated her with any unwanted attention either. So, that wasn't it; she was making excuses to be alone with me.

I'll take it.

ɛ♦

And so, that's how we found ourselves sitting across from each other at my kitchen table, eating Mexican takeout from Bitty's Burrito Bar. We ping-ponged questions back and forth, getting to know each other, with her occasional, teasing reminders, to not hesitate, to be honest, to not stall.

"How many cats do you have?" she asked, finishing the last of her burrito.

"Four."

"So, you're a crazy cat man, huh?"

I considered it. I might have been crazy, and I definitely liked cats, so I shrugged with my hands. "Yeah, ya could say that."

"What are their names?"

"Cheryl, Tara, Jennifer, and Jessica."

She bit her inner cheek with unabashed amusement. "Let me guess … You named them all after celebrities you used to jack off to."

I grinned, barking a surprised laugh. "Ooh, good guess, but …" I shook my head. "Nah, try again."

"They're named after your favorite housewives from one of those reality shows?"

I laughed again, not bothering to point out that I don't own a TV. "God, you're just *so close*."

"Really?"

"Not even a little."

She threw a chip across the table at me. "Okay, wiseass, fine," she said with a laughing grin. "Where the hell did you come up with those names? Be honest," she said, pointing a finger at me.

A momentary flash of memory hit me, one of my mother reprimanding me for lying about where I had been all night. She had known I was lying and known I had been up to no good, thanks to the evidential spray paint residue on my sneakers. Her stern finger pointed, while her pretty blue eyes revealed every question of where she had gone wrong. I'd stared, wide-eyed and terrified, as though that finger could pull the very life from me if I even tried to tell her another lie. As though those eyes alone could break my heart.

I had to squeeze my eyes shut to get rid of it. To get the image of my feckin' mother out of my head.

"Right," I said, opening my eyes and seeing, not Mam, but the girl I was sleeping with, and I quietly answered, "They're named after my ex-girlfriends."

Her mouth fell open, her eyes displaying the exact amount of shock I expected. This was the part where most women would have taken that as their own red flag and run away, thinking I was a total lunatic. But God, not Snow. She closed her mouth, smiling with that wicked excitement.

"Oh Ireland, you really *are* a weirdo," she said softly. "I like it."

"You would," I teased, throwing a tortilla chip back at her.

She caught it and took a bite. "Ask me something now."

"Will you stay over tonight?"

"Yes."

"Good." I smiled, and we finished our dinner.

She cleared the table; I put away the leftovers. I washed the dishes; she dried them and put them away. She told me to tie her wrists with the dish towel; I did. She told me to bend her over the table we had just eaten on, told me to fuck her; I gladly obliged.

On the second night of knowing her, the second night of feasting upon her body, I took in our ease of working as a team. I wasn't sure I had ever experienced something like it before and thinking about those four ex-girlfriends, I wondered if they would have been different had we been *there*. You know … *A team.*

I flipped her over on the hand-me-down table like a tattooed Thanksgiving feast, and I stared, thinking about the past and how this present was already so different. I watched as those barbells in her nipples glistened under the lights in the basement ceiling; they wiggled and bobbed as she breathed, as she lazily toyed with their gemmed ends. I swallowed, allowing my hands to roam over her decorated skin. Along her sides, indenting at her hips, out with her waist, and down, down over her slender legs.

"I can tell when you're doing it," she said in a soft, drowsy voice, eyes almost closed.

"Doin' what?" I asked, my words scratching at my throat.

"Thinking." And slowly, she pulled herself up into a seated position, legs dangling over the edge of the table. Her bejeweled nipples tickled over my chest as she tipped her head back and pursed her lips. One hand reached up, tugged at my beard, and I bent, touching my mouth lightly to hers. Leaning back, she held my face between her hands, and said, "You disappear for a few seconds. Your eyes cross a little, and you get a little line right … here." She touched her finger between my brows.

"Hmm," I grunted, and that was something else. Her ability to know things, to know me. What could have been different if I had been more predictable to *them*, if they had been—

"You're doing it again," Snow said. There was something sad in her voice. Something that said she might care for me as something more than just a guy to fuck until she got bored.

"I'm allowed to think," I said in a low voice that, for a moment, I hoped was threatening. Who the hell did she think she was, telling me what to do. Telling me when to think.

She shook her head, and my temper ignited. Just a little spark, but it was there. "Don't," she said, her voice soft and soothing. "Not like that. Not with me."

Not like that. Not with me.

I repeated the words in my head, calming the anger, the need to beat and berate myself. I found her, found her crystal blue eyes against their canvas of black and white, and I wrapped my arms around her and pulled her from the table.

I carried that woman, with her legs around my waist, to the shower. I took my time as I washed her, and then she washed me—*teamwork*. And after, as she used one of the toothbrushes my mother had dropped off for me, she noticed that I dyed my hair with the same stuff she used.

"We could have hair-dying parties," she laughed excitedly, her mouth full of toothpaste.

"Oh, great," I grumbled sarcastically, but I smiled around my own toothbrush. Because it was those little things that made me wonder, made my heart beat just a little faster.

Little, *hopeful*, things that didn't really feel so little at all.

We got into bed, naked and comfortable, and with her head against my chest, she traced the outlines of one tattoo: the Celtic family tree I shared with my brothers.

"I like this one," she said.

I nodded. "I do too."

"A lot of your other tattoos are kind of, um …"

"Stupid?" I offered with a grin. It wasn't a lie. I'd gotten many of my tattoos in the basements of friends' houses, most of them badly done and attributed to something ridiculous I no longer cared about.

She hesitated. "Well, yeah, but I can't say mine are much better. This one, though …" She traced her finger in a circle around the tree. "This one is pretty. You can tell it has meaning."

"It does." I smiled, shivering a little as that finger kept on spinning around, around, around. She memorized its knotted lines, tracing the vessels of my heart, the foundation of my soul.

As the dark settled over the room and we were together falling into sleep, she broke the silence with her voice.

"Who lives upstairs?" she asked.

"My grandmother."

"Was that your idea, or was it pushed on you, like your job?"

My breath stalled, held in my lungs, and I scowled in the darkness. Quick anger prickling away at me. "Why do you wanna know?"

"Relax, Ireland. I'm not judging."

I sighed, and the tension dissipated. "It was *asked* of me, not *pushed*. I could have said no, to the apartment and the job, but I went with it."

"To not be a disappointment?"

There was that word. The little devil on my back, the demon whispering in my ear. "*Yep*."

"We *will* work on that, okay?"

My jaw tightened, my body stilled, and the moisture in my mouth was dried up instantly.

It wasn't the first time a woman had offered to help me, to make me less, *me. Cheryl* had turned me into a science experiment of the heart. It hadn't worked, and I was left to live as an even bigger disappointment.

I should have been afraid when Snow said those words—"*We will work on that*." I should have taken that as another red flag.

But I didn't. And maybe that should have been a red flag in itself.

"Okay," I croaked out. "Sure."

"Good."

She raised up on an elbow and kissed me before rolling over. She guided me to do the same, to spoon her with my arm wrapped around her naked waist with my dick nestled against her arse. She was freezing, always seemed to be, but my body engulfed her in warmth, and she sighed.

Teamwork.

CHAPTER FOUR
STOLEN TEA & OLD WOMEN

I woke up to empty arms. The side of the bed she had occupied was made, and her clothes were missing from the floor. This was a big no-no in my mental list of sleepover rules, and I jumped out of bed with my blood sizzling in my veins.

The bitch had left. That pierced, tattooed little bitch had said all that shite about thinking and fixing, and then she left.

I muttered curse words, as I threw a t-shirt over my head. I muttered some more as I threw on a pair of sweatpants, and my fists clenched as I moved into the kitchen to throw open a cabinet door. It bounced on its hinges and hit the wall as I grabbed a mug. Then there came the voices from above my head. Granny's laughter. Slippered feet shuffling along the floor.

"What the feckin' hell?" I said loudly to the ceiling, and I slammed the mug down on the counter, and headed for the door leading to the stairs.

Taking them two at a time, I swung the door open into my grandmother's kitchen, hung a right into the outdated living room, and found myself looking at Granny in her robe, sitting next to Snow, on the couch.

Snow was wearing my shirt. No pants.

Where the hell had her clothes gone? And more importantly, what the feck was she doing, sitting there with my feckin' grandmother?

"What the hell are ya doin'?" I said, flabbergasted. I hadn't intended for my voice to sound as though someone was squeezing my nuts, and the two women immediately stopped their chattering. My old Irish grandmother and the chick I was banging turned to me, and they laughed. "And what the hell is so goddamn funny?"

Granny continued her giggling, slapping a hand over her terry-clothed knee. Snow held a hand over her mouth, muffling her own laughter until she could speak.

"Oh God, Ireland," she said, struggling to catch her breath. "You should see your face right now. You look like you're going to shit yourself."

"Snow," I warned, looking between her and my grandmother. "Ya really shouldn't be up here."

"Oh really? Are you trying to tell me what to do?" She cocked her head, smirking. Challenging me.

My lips curled into a snarl. "Don't you—"

Granny creaked off the couch. She smoothed her robe over her thighs, and shuffled over to me, patting my chest. "Ah, calm that temper of yours, Ryan. Your lady friend and I were just havin' a wee chat and settin' to have a cup o' tea. Would y'like one yourself?"

"What? *Tea*? Are you kiddin'—"

"No, I'm not kiddin'. Come on, my boy; it'll calm those nerves of yours."

"Ehm, fine. Sure." The muscles in my jaw eased, but my glare remained on the tiny feckin' woman on the couch.

"Granny, I can get it. You sit," Snow said, jumping up to stop the old woman, and my breath hissed through my nose at the sound of her using her family title.

Granny turned, pointing a knobby finger at the raven-haired girl that I couldn't take my eyes off, and shook her head. "You are a *guest* in my house, young lady. Sit yourself down. I won't be a minute."

I grumbled, "You'll be a lot more than a minute."

My old grandmother, with her Q-tip hair and weathered skin, grinned up at me. "Watch it, boy. I can still drink ya under the table. Don't forget who wears the pants 'round this house."

Snow's mouth twisted around a smile as I rolled my eyes. "Ya haven't had a drink in more years than me, old woman."

"And I've been alive a lot longer, my boy. You kids and your *light beer*." She tsked and waved her hands dismissively. "All a bunch of *lightweights*."

I laughed easily as she began to totter her way toward the kitchen. "I've never had a light beer in my life!" I said to the back of her head.

"That's my boy," she said with a light laugh before disappearing behind the wall.

Then, with my grandmother out of the room, I turned back to Snow. "Seriously, Snow. What the feck are ya doin' up here? And Christ, couldn't ya have put on some feckin' pants? You're embarrassin' both of us. My grandmother doesn't need to see—"

"So, your accent gets thicker around your family, huh?" Those soft, pink lips smiled sweetly, and I shook my head, chasing away the image of kissing them.

"You're changin' the—"

"It's so fucking hot," she purred, and sashayed toward me, placing her hands on my chest, and she stood on her toes. Her lips pursed into a fish-face and without a second thought, I accepted the invitation, touching my mouth to hers.

Don't forget you're mad. Don't forget she's stepping over lines. Don't forget she's wrong, don't forget you're right, don't forget you like her, don't forget you're going to feck this all up.

"I woke up, you were still sleeping, and I was in the mood for tea. You didn't have any, so I figured a little old Irish grandmother would have some." She circled her arms around my waist. Her cheek pressed against my chest. My heart beat louder and harder with every breath she took.

"So, what was your plan?"

"Plan?" She pulled away to look up at me.

"Yeah. Were ya just gonna come up here to steal from an old woman you've never met?" I quirked an eyebrow, the endless cycle of internal chatter dulling in my brain.

She smiled, rolling her crystal eyes playfully. "Come *on*, Ireland. I heard her moving around up here, so I came up to *ask*. Then, she invited me to have a cup with her. She also offered to make some toast and eggs too, if you'd like to scold her for that, but I'm not a breakfast person."

Neither was I.

All those little things.

The annoyance was gone, the thoughts were gone. The tension was released, and my muscles relaxed. "Well … All right, but seriously, ya could have at least put on some pants."

"I threw my clothes in your laundry basket. They're a little, uh, *dirty*, and none of yours would've fit me." She lifted the shirt, flashing me yesterday's panties. "I had the sense to cover my ass, though, don't worry."

I shot a look toward the kitchen and pushed the shirt down over her.

"Is Granny one of those River Canyon Prudes?" she teased, giggling.

"Well, no, but—"

She smiled, wrapping her arms around me again. "You don't bring girls back here much, huh?"

"I don't bring girls here, period."

Her face froze. Staring at me as she took that in. Then she said, "But you brought me here?"

I pushed a hand through my sleep-mussed hair. "Yeah, well, ya made me an offer I couldn't refuse, and I didn't expect ya to be meetin' members of my family without my approval first."

"I don't need your *approval*, Ireland," she scolded gently. Her features hardened, but her arms tightened. So many contradictions—just like winter. "I do what I want."

"Yeah, I see that," I said, my voice gruff and firm.

She leaned forward, kissed my chest. "You should, too."

My mouth opened to tell her to butt out of my personal business, to keep her opinions to herself, but she stood on her toes to press her lips against mine and unable to contain myself, I pulled her against me. With a little whimpered moan, her tongue swiped over my lower lip just as Granny came tottering back in with a clattering tray of tea cups, milk, and a bowl of sugar lumps.

"All right, there's no reason to be gettin' a ride right where I can see ya."

"Oh, for Christ's sake, Granny," I groaned under my breath, feeling instantly like a sixteen-year-old kid and not a thirty-year-old man. Snow looked up at me with a questioning glance. "She thinks we're gonna fuck in the middle of her living room."

"And here, I was under the impression you thought highly of me," she said to my grandmother, grinning, and Granny shook her head.

"It's not you, dear. It's that one I don't trust," she said, and while her eyes sparkled playfully in the sunlight, her lips lifted into a half-smile.

"Very nice," I grumbled, fighting back my own grin.

I stepped away from Snow, grabbing the tray from my grandmother's shaky hands, and brought it over to the coffee table. Snow excused herself, saying she'd be back in just a minute before heading downstairs, and I tensed at the thought of being alone with Granny and whatever criticisms she might've been suppressing.

I raked a hand through my hair, diverting my eyes to the ceiling. The slow-moving fan in the center of the room. The cobwebs that I should really wipe away. "Ehm, I'm sorry about—"

Granny clucked her tongue, tapped me on the arm. "Ryan, my boy, you're a grown man. Do y'honestly believe I never thought you'd bring a woman home?"

Another hand raked through my hair. "Ah, well … No, but—"

"Y'know, I like her. She's a bit eccentric, and very … *decorated*, I should say, but I think she complements ya, wouldn't ya say?"

And what in the hell was I supposed to say to that?

Because, I mean, on one hand, I didn't necessarily disagree. Our dynamic was good, the sex was better than good, and the sleep I got with her was the best I had in years. Possibly ever.

Teamwork.

But then, on the other hand, we were talking about a woman I had only screwed a few times over the course of a couple days. We weren't together—hell, we weren't even friends, as far as I could tell. We weren't really *anything*, and there she was, introducing herself to my grandmother. Asking her for tea, and thinking she had some sort of say in how I lived my feckin' life.

So, did she complement me, or was she simply poking her nose where it didn't belong? Forcing herself in and overstepping her bounds?

So many feckin' red flags.

"Granny, that tea smells amazing." I turned at Snow's voice as she emerged from the basement, wiping wet hands on the shirt she wore. "You need a hand towel in your bathroom," she said, turning to me with a glint in her eye. "We'll go shopping today. And maybe we could grab a few pillows, too?"

"What the hell's wrong with my pillows?" I asked, as I sat down in the recliner. Snow filled two cups of tea from the pot, before climbing onto my lap. Instinct had me put my arm around her, and her arse fit comfortably over my cock with a familiarity that said I was going to have her later.

"Uh, nothing, except that they smell like they've been around for way longer than their intended lifespan."

"They smell fine," I grumbled, and took a cup from her, sipping lightly.

Snow laughed, and I shot her a questioning glance.

"I wish I had a camera right now. I'd take a picture and remember you and your dainty little teacup forever."

"Forever, huh," I muttered against the brim of my cup, and with that, it didn't feel so much like overstepping at all.

"Yeah," she said on a shallow breath. "Forever."

Such a little word: *forever*.

Little things that didn't feel so little at all.

Granny covered her mouth, failing to conceal her smile. "Oh, my boy, I *do* like her."

I was so feckin' screwed.

CHAPTER FIVE
ESSENTIAL OILS & TRUE COLORS

She convinced me to call out sick, and I *never* called out. Hell, I would spit out my lungs before I didn't go to work, but there I was, the day before Christmas Eve, coughing into the phone and telling my boss I wasn't feeling well. Because *apparently*, I had to go shopping for hand towels and pillows.

And I grumbled and grunted, protesting every step of the feckin' way as she pushed the cart through Harold's, River Canyon's only department store, tossing things in that she felt I needed. But did I take a damn thing out? Did I put anything back? Nope, because y'know, the more I thought about it, the more I felt there was something sort of nice about giving someone that wasn't Mam or Da permission to take control.

Christ knew I couldn't control the *important shite* myself. I had failed too many times to know that for certain, and so, I had handed the reins over to my parents. Letting them handle the majority of my finances, my schedule. We had a system, and while some might call it "dysfunctional," it worked for me—giving them that control.

Hell, I thrived on it.

Being thirty years old and answering willingly to my Mam and Da wasn't exactly something to brag about, was it? But I hadn't been looking for any brownie points; I was looking for *help*. And for two years, I had convinced myself that was the only place I would find it.

But then …

Well, there was *this*.

Snow and her shopping cart of pillows and hand towels.

Having a woman decide which soaps to put in the kitchen and bathroom? It was so feckin' *domestic*, so much like playing house, and dammit, it was kind of nice. It was something I never quite had before, not even when living with ex-girlfriends. With them, it had been a constant game of Tug O' War, pushing and pulling until one of us finally snapped. But with Snow, it felt *good* and *right*, and so, behind her back, when I wasn't grumbling, I was grinning. Watching her bounce through the aisles, smiling at me over her shoulder. She looked so genuinely happy, so … so … *invested.*

She turned around, holding up a pack of … something. "You're doing it again," she said lightly, and I cocked a grin.

"Doin' what?"

"That thinking thing."

I shrugged, stuffing my hands into the pockets of my jeans. "It's what I do; I *think.*"

"I noticed," she teased with a smile, reaching out to tug gently at my beard. It had become an affectionate little thing, and I feckin' loved it.

"Anyway, what do you think of this?" she asked and held up the pack of things.

I shrugged again. "Ehm … what the hell is it?"

"Seriously?"

I squinted at the package in her hands, and then shook my head. "Yeah, I have no feckin' clue what those are."

"Well, *that* explains a lot …" she teased under her breath as she dropped it into the cart.

Cocking my head, I asked, "So, are you gonna tell me what they are, or not?"

Snow sighed. "They're essential oils, Ireland."

An immediate rush of blood to the groin. "Oh, ehm … right. Didn't think this was *that* kind of store, but I'm down for any—"

She threw her head back and laughed. "Oh my God, *no*! They're *scent* oils! You know, to make your apartment smell good?"

Deflated and only a little less turned on, I scowled. "What are you sayin'?"

"I'm saying that, you've clearly never lived with a woman before, because your apartment smells like a man who smokes like a chimney and has too many cats," she teased, standing on her toes to kiss me. My brows furrowed, and she stopped mid-way to my mouth. "What's that look for?"

"I've lived with women before," I stated bluntly, fighting to keep that vile taste from filling my mouth.

She tugged at my beard again. "Your granny doesn't count," she said, and kissed me in the middle of the aisle, shushing my words before they began. Shushing my thoughts before they could head in the direction of ex-girlfriends and disappointments.

I wondered if she felt it, too. That whole *teamwork* thing.

Snow turned around and resumed her pushing. I kept a distance to watch her arse rock in her tight black jeans, wishing we were back in my smelly apartment, when I was suddenly startled by ...

"Ryan?"

And with the intrusion of that voice, I was reminded that she had dragged me to the department store my brother worked at.

With a concealed deep breath, I turned slowly to face him. "Hey Seanie," I said, feigning enthusiasm with a grin and a shove against his shoulder.

Feckin' small towns.

"What are you doin' here?" he asked, cocking his head questioningly. But Sean was observant, and it didn't take him long to notice that woman, standing at no more than five feet tall and looking an awful lot like someone I'd find myself wrapped around. He smirked knowingly, wiggling his brows at me.

"Knock it off," I grumbled under my breath.

"I didn't say anything," he said with a gentle shrug, but that smirk hadn't disappeared.

"Cut it out," I warned, pointing a finger at his face.

"Wha—"

"Hey Ireland?" Snow called, and Sean's smirk widened into a grin.

"*Ireland*, huh? That's … sweet," he teased, and I elbowed him in the side before turning to look at her.

"Yeah?"

She was eyeing a two-pack of oven mitts with scrutiny and turned around to notice I had fallen behind a few steps. She threw the mitts into the cart and bounded over to wrap herself around my arm.

"Hey, I'm Snow," she introduced herself, thrusting a hand at my twin, and he accepted with a kind smile.

"Sean," he said, and bumped my shoulder with his hand. "I'm this arsehole's brother. How come I've never seen you before?"

"Just moved in. I'm the new tattoo artist at Canvas & Ink," she said, casually smiling as she squeezed my arm tighter to her chest. She looked up at me with a soul-soothing affection, the way she would've if we were a couple. But in that moment, her jaw dropped, and she looked between his face and mine, and she pointed a finger with a grin. "Oh my God, Ireland, you have a twin!"

The black hair, tattoos, and excessive workouts couldn't keep us from sharing the same smile, same chin, same height, same voice. Not that I had ever purposely tried to change my appearance to be different from Sean; our personalities did that for us just fine.

"What was your first clue?" I asked, looking at her with a smirk.

"You have the same eyes," she said, smiling up at Sean, and then me.

"Yeah, we've gotten that before," Sean laughed, and he was right—we had. Hell, there had even been a time when folks couldn't tell us apart, as the stereotype of identical twins goes. But studying him now, I couldn't see it anymore. Mine were a little more weathered, thanks to all those years of smoking and once-upon-a-time drinking. I had seen too much, been *hurt* too much, and his were still the eyes of someone who had yet to have his heart truly broken.

But Christ, that Snow … She saw something else.

❦

She didn't tell me until we were in her car, the little old orange VW Beetle that I had to fold myself three times to get into. I dwarfed the feckin' thing, and I shook my head at the absurdity of sitting in it and made a comment about finally knowing what it was like to ride around in a clown car.

"Oh, shut up," she laughed, gripping the steering wheel underneath her fingerless gloves. "I love this car." She patted the wheel affectionately.

"I didn't say it wasn't a good car. Although … it *is* a feckin' miracle the thing even runs," I said with a chuckle. "I'm just sayin', you're the shortest woman I've ever known, and you fit just fine, but me? I'm gonna need a chiropractor on call after I get out of here."

"The shortest you've *ever* known?" she laughed.

"*Easily*," I said, my smile stretching. "I mean, you have to be, what? Four-two?"

She gasped. "Four-foot-ten, thank you very much! Jesus … You're not *that* much taller than me," she said with a playful roll of her eyes.

"I'm almost a foot and a half taller than you!" I laughed heartily. "*Definitely* the shortest woman I've ever known."

Snow looked over at me, caught my eye and swallowed as her smile faded. "You know ..." But then she shook her head and turned her gaze back on the road. She sighed heavily, her fingers gripped the wheel, but she refrained from continuing.

"What?" I asked, gently prying.

"No, it's just that ... you have such tired eyes, you know that? Your brother does, too."

"What?" I asked, taken aback by the observation.

She shrugged, keeping her eyes on the road. "I don't know ... I was just thinking about it. It's funny, because when I first looked at the two of you, I couldn't tell you were even twins. Maybe because of the hair, or maybe the beard threw me off—I don't know. But then, I got a good look at his eyes, and I saw the same thing I see in yours."

My elbow tucked against the window ledge and my hand pushed through my hair. "And what did you see?"

"Like you're both carrying the world on your shoulders. Like ... you share a burden or something."

"That's quite an assessment to make just by lookin' at someone's eyes," I said, a tight laugh forcing its way up my throat.

"Yeah," she said quietly.

I glanced over at her as she snubbed out the conversation by turning up the radio, and I was instantly struck with thoughts about fate. Because in that moment, Phil Collins's rendition of "True Colors" was playing, and as she reached for the radio dial, I put my hand over hers, stopping her.

"Wait."

She bubbled with laughter. "You're joking, right? I didn't take you for a Philly C. kind of guy."

"I'm not," I shot at her, more defensive than I should have been over a stupid song. "Just ... keep it on."

I was granted a total of thirteen seconds to listen to the song, and I took in the lyrics about darkness and feeling small, and not being afraid to let your true colors show. Snow glanced over at my intense gaze, trained on the dashboard of her little clown car, and she shook her head, switching the station to something louder, something more *us*, and Godsmack's "Voodoo" filled the car.

"I couldn't watch you do that to yourself," she laughed with a twinkle in her crystalline eyes.

"Thanks for savin' me," I said, laughing with her, but my thoughts were elsewhere. My thoughts were on what she had said about my eyes, they were on the lyrics of that song, and I wondered what else she saw—what else she'd *see*.

Would it be something she'd have to fix?

Would it be something that would make her leave?

Or would it be something else entirely?

Hell, maybe even something good.

₭

Later that night, after putting the new sheets on the bed, Snow jumped on to starfish over its surface.

"I love the feeling of new sheets. They're just made to be ruined," she sighed, stretching her long limbs out, corner to corner. Toes pointed, fingers spread. "Come here, Ireland. Christen them with me."

I shook my head. "Dinner first."

"Nuh-uh, I don't think so." She rolled over, grabbed for my hand, and tugged.

"It's gonna get cold," I protested, but the breaded chicken cutlets and potatoes on the table went forgotten as I dropped to the bed.

"Fuck chicken," she laughed, pushing her hands into my hair and snagging my lower lip between her teeth. "Can I have you for dinner instead?"

Groaning, I kissed her, wrapping my arms around her waist. "Why doesn't it surprise me that you'd be into cannibalism?"

She pushed me to my back, lean thighs positioned on either side of my hips. I looked up her torso, over her tattooed arms and shoulders. How she could manage in that chilly room in nothing but a pair of underwear and a tank top, I had no idea, but I was grateful for it. I pictured those glittering nipples, wanted them in my mouth. To feel that cool metal on my teeth, gliding the slippery ends over my tongue.

"What are you thinking?" she asked, looking down at me.

Goddammit. I grinned. "I'm thinkin' we should let dinner get cold. I'm thinkin' … I can practically see your tits through this thing, and I want them in my mouth. I'm thinkin' you should take care of *this* …" She let out a moan as I slid my hands under the thin black material, circled her hips with my fingers, pulled her down against my strained erection.

"I *guess* I could do that," she said, leaning forward to press her lips to mine. "But first, ask me what *I'm* thinking."

I grinned against her mouth. "What are you thinkin'?" I obliged, gruff words heating her lips.

Snow flattened her hands over my chest, slid them up to my shoulders and kissed me lightly. Lips barely touching, so featherlight. "I want to go to your family's house for Christmas."

My hard-on shriveled to raisin proportions at the thought of her attending a Kinney Family Christmas. The sheer thought of bringing a girl home, one that I had only been fucking for a few days, seemed foolish. Reckless. Disappointing. *Typical Ryan.* It was bad enough she had invited herself to meet my Granny, and coincidentally happened to be there when seeing my brother. I just *knew* the two of them would eventually tell Mam and Da that I was sleeping with the new girl in town. But *Christmas*?

I laughed, because, she had to be joking. I laughed, and waited for her to join in. I laughed, but I laughed alone.

"Come on. You're jokin', right?"

She leaned away, and as she absentmindedly pulled at the hem of my t-shirt, she said, "I'm serious Ryan. I don't know anybody here, and I really don't want to spend Christmas alone. I've never spent Christmas alone."

I watched the faintest forlorn glint flicker over her gaze, and I let my guilty conscience needle away at me. "Ah, Christ …" I sat up, putting my chest against hers. I could feel the pebbled nipples through her shirt. Felt the cold metal of her jewelry, seeping through the fabric. "I understand that, but I can't take you to my family's house for Christmas, Snow. What would I say to them?"

"You can say anything," she said, her gaze meeting mine.

"But you're not even my girlfriend." I eyed her with uncertainty. "I don't think?"

Her arms encircled my neck, her hands resting lazily against my back. "I don't think I can ever be your girlfriend, Ireland."

I was taken aback, stunned even, by the admission. "Is it really that hard to be with me?" I laughed nervously.

"It's not hard to be with you at all. I *like* being around you—a lot, actually—"

"So, what's the problem?"

"It's just that …" Her voice trailed off and toyed with the hem of my shirt.

"Just, what?"

She sighed. "Leaving you might be the problem."

"You expect to leave me? Who *plans* on that kinda thing?"

Snow looked toward the window, seeking the air it controlled. "Sometimes, Ryan, no matter how much you plan, no matter how long you've been together, people still leave. You can't keep other people from breaking your heart. You can hope they'll stay, hope they'll do exactly what you'd like them to, but in the end, sometimes you're just meant to deal with the pain of losing them." Her voice ebbed and flowed, rising and falling with tiny bursts of hidden emotion, and I wondered …

"Did someone hurt you?" I asked, squeezing her hips firmly in my hands.

She shook her head, shook away the buried pain. "We're not talking about me," she said.

"Then what are we talking about?"

"We're talking about cats."

I allowed a laugh at that. "*Cats*?"

"Yes! Cats! Look at what you do with your girlfriends Ryan. They break your heart, they turn out to be someone else, and you go out and get a cat to name after them. Because you don't allow yourself to deal with the pain. You get a replacement, and one you can control."

She kissed the lips that didn't—*wouldn't*—kiss back. "Ryan, if I'm someone who's meant to break your heart, or if you're someone who's meant to break mine … I really don't want to become a cat."

My nostrils twitched, my lips made the move to frown. My throat strained around a growing lump, and I instantly regretted telling her that truth, instantly regretted telling her the reason for the names.

She didn't know my history, and those words … Those words were harsh. They were as cold as her hands, chilling the tattooed skin on my back through my thin t-shirt. Every bone in my body screamed in agony, warning me to shove her off, get out of the bed, and find warmth, just to ward off the hypothermia she was causing.

But the thing about those words was, they were also true; that thing about wanting to regain control, knowing deep down I could never handle it. That thing about not allowing myself to deal with how it—*relationships*—ended. The cats *were* replacements for the things I had loved—*thought* I loved—and couldn't have. The things that had shut me out, things that had run away. Snow was the only person to see it for what it was, the only person to acknowledge how truly nuts my quirk was, and she hadn't run away from it. She had wrapped her arms around my neck, kissed my lips, and accepted it.

And that acceptance …

Well, I didn't shove her off, because of that. And because something told me I wasn't destined to break her heart, and she wasn't destined to break mine.

"Okay," I accepted, wrapping my arms around her back, pressing her hard against me.

"Okay?" She tipped her forehead against mine. The hoop that hugged the center of her lower lip clacked against her teeth as she bit down.

"You can have Christmas with me," I said, ignoring that small voice in my head as it whispered, *"Disappointment."*

CHAPTER SIX
CHRISTMAS & SUBMISSION

I parked Granny's old Lincoln outside of my parents' house and turned to Snow.

She wanted to impress them. She wouldn't admit to it, but she didn't have to. She had curled her hair, worn a dress ... Hell, even her makeup was done in a way that made her look a little less like *Elvira*, and as if that wasn't enough, she had even taken over my kitchen to bake a feckin' pie.

"What?" she asked, when she caught me staring.

"Nothin'." The corners of my mouth lifted, and she gave me a gentle shove.

"No, come on. What are you smiling about?"

"Ooh, Ryan's gettin' into trouble ..." Granny laughed from the backseat.

"Watch it, old woman," I said with a light chuckle, and I turned to Snow. "I just think it's kinda nice that you're makin' an effort."

"An effort?" she asked, narrowing her eyes.

"Yeah," I said with a nod. "I mean, obviously you're trying to impress my family."

Her pale skin flushed. "Don't look into it, Ireland. It's *Christmas*. I didn't want to show up looking like *The Crypt Keeper*. So, stop trying to turn it into something it's not, okay?"

And I tried not to look into it—really, I did. But as I watched the nervous movements of her hands and the telltale bite against her lip, I couldn't help the webs my mind dared to weave. And I continued to observe the gentle way she helped Granny from the car. The way she clung to her pie tin and my arm as we climbed the creaking porch steps. And then, when she took a deep breath and smiled bravely at me before I reached out to grab at the doorknob of my childhood home, my mind dared me to do something I hadn't done in a long time: *I hoped.*

My hand barely grazed the handle when the door flew open to reveal my sister-in-law, Kinsey. She smiled at me, at Granny, and then, she smiled something a little more curious at Snow. Her eyes glinted, glancing up at me with a little teasing smirk.

"Hey Ry, you brought a friend?" Her mouth twitched around the word "friend," as though she knew it meant more than how she said it, and I had this sinking feeling that it was going to be a long feckin' night.

I harrumphed and placed a hand between Snow's shoulder blades. "Kinsey, this is Snow. Snow, this is my sister-in-law."

"Ah, the new girl at the tattoo place," Kinsey said with an acknowledging nod, and she looked up at me. "Doesn't take you long, huh?"

"Feck off," I growled, and I chuckled good-naturedly as I bent to wrap her in a big hug. "Merry Christmas, Kins."

"Merry Christmas," she said, wrapping her arms around my neck and kissing my cheek. She looked over at Granny and smiled. "Merry Christmas to you too, Granny!"

"And to you as well, m'dear," the old woman said with a smile and a pat on the arm.

"You're Sean's wife," Snow stated the moment Kinsey was released from my grasp, stepping around me and into the house I grew up in, as though she had been there a thousand times before.

Kinsey smiled. "No, I'm married to Patrick."

Snow turned to me, mouth open in shock. "Ireland, you didn't tell me you have another brother!"

I thought to point out the obvious—that we had known each other for less than a week, and that the majority of our time together had been spent having sex. But, I didn't want to embarrass her, didn't want to show myself as the disappointment that I am, and I just smiled.

"Ah, yep, he's—"

"Now, the party's here!" As though he had heard me talking about him, that older brother announced his presence with his overpowering voice, walking into the room and heading straight toward Granny.

"Oh, get the hell outta my face, Paddy. Where are my great-grandbabies?" she said, but she laughed as he engulfed her frail little body with his arms and kissed her on the cheek.

"Hey old woman, ya gotta get through me before you can get to them," he said, kissing her again. Then he stood, his attention diverted as he gently squeezed her shoulder. "Meg and Erin are in the kitchen with Mam and Da. Go make sure they don't ruin dinner. Last I checked, they had Erin usin' the blender."

Erin was an infant.

I snorted. "You're a feckin' idiot," I said with a laughing grin and a shake of my head.

"But somehow, we manage to put up with him, anyway," Granny said, patting him in the center of the chest.

And with that, she tottered away to shower her great-grandchildren with hugs, kisses and money, leaving us alone in the living room. Patrick pulled me into a hug, clapping his hand against my back, but he kept a curious eye on Snow the whole time.

Kinsey spoke before I even had a chance. "Babe, Ryan brought a *friend*," she said in that teasing voice she had used my entire life. She wiggled her brows up at him, and I glowered down at her. "This is Snow. You know, the new girl at Canvas & Ink?"

Patrick turned to look at Snow, and he smiled. "Ah, right. I heard ya were in town," and then, he bent to kiss her cheek. "Merry Christmas. It's nice to finally meet you. I've been meaning to stop in and welcome ya, but I haven't had the chance."

"No, he's too busy harassing me at work." Kinsey rolled her eyes over to her husband.

"What do you do?" Snow asked, eyes bouncing between them.

"I run McKenna's Delicatessen," Kinsey answered.

"So, you're the gal to go to if I ever have a hankering for a pastrami sub?"

"Oh, hell yeah! And we also—"

"Don't do it," Patrick said with a warning shake of his head. "She's the reason I'm wakin' up an hour early to get more time in at the gym."

"Nobody's *makin'* ya eat a pound of potato salad every feckin' day," I groaned with a shove against his shoulder.

Snow exchanged a look with Kinsey, some unspoken words were said between them, and the two of them laughed. "Okay, so what do *you* do?" Snow asked him, and Patrick smiled, his symmetrical dimples emerging.

"I'm a cop."

And with that, I waited for the twinkle that women got in their eyes when looking at him; my older brother who had made the best of a disappointing situation. He was the charmer, the taller and more handsome brother. He had the dimples, he had the eyes. He had the laugh, he had the uniform. And no, I wasn't jealous of him, but I also knew that when standing next to him, I came in at second best. It wasn't even pessimism. Nah, it was *realism*, and I knew my place on the Kinney Brother Pyramid.

But not Snow.

She didn't get that glint when looking at his unshaven face or those *dreamy* eyes that Kinsey had always gone completely gaga over from the moment they knew that boys and girls were different. Nope, not Snow. She just smiled at him, like he wasn't anything other than my brother married to the literal girl next door.

But more importantly, she didn't look at him the way I had seen her look at me, and that felt like something. Something I could hope for. Something less like a disappointment, and more like something I wanted. Hell, maybe even something I *needed*.

༄

The last time I had brought a woman home to meet the family had been four years ago. The perfect summer afternoon for a backyard barbeque. The last one Patrick's ex-wife, Christine, would attend.

Cheryl and I had been together for six months, and with her and her bouncing blonde ponytail by my side, I walked through the gate feeling like I had won the feckin' lottery. That day Mam, Da, Patrick, Sean, and Christine's jaws all hit the ground, seeing that Ivy League princess with her unmarked skin on my arm. They asked her how she managed to get strapped to *a guy like me*, asked me how I managed to *get so lucky*.

I didn't have an answer to that question, because I had asked myself that every single day for the year and a half we spent together.

And as Snow and I moved through to the kitchen. I wondered what Mam was thinking when she got her first look at her and the ring piercing her septum. I wondered what Da was saying to himself when he caught sight of the tattoos on her fingers, tipped with freshly painted black nails.

I braced myself as Mam handed Patrick's baby daughter Erin to his older daughter Meghan, and I closed my hands around themselves as she and Da made their way over to us.

"Ryan!" Mam reprimanded me, swatting gently at my arm. "Why didn't ya say y'were bringin' someone home?"

Snow shot a disapproving look up at me. "Ryan!" she hissed, nerves and embarrassment flushing her cheeks, and I shrugged my shoulders, already slumped with apprehension.

"Sorry," I mumbled, and introduced my mother and father to Snow.

And I waited.

I waited for the darkened glances of disappointment that she wasn't the blonde Harvard graduate they had once known. The one I drove away. The one that kicked me out. I waited for the slightest twitch of an upper lip, the disgust that I had brought home another girl with dyed black hair and tattoos to match mine.

But Mam just smiled at Snow, never once displaying judgment or ridicule, and she embraced her in true Helen Kinney fashion. Her arms wrapped around her shoulders as she said, "It's lovely to meet ya, Snow, and what a gorgeous name y'have!"

Snow's eyes shot toward mine, her anxiety dulling the gleam I usually found in them, and I smiled encouragingly. "U-um … Thank you, Mrs. Kinney, and I'm sorry for not reminding Ryan to tell you I was coming. It was a really last-minute decision, and I guess I had figured he would have said something to you beforehand," Snow said. "If it's too much trouble, don't—"

Mam waved a hand with her signature carefree smile, gripping Snow's shoulder. "Don't y'worry, dear. I can easily make a space for ya at the table."

Da, a man of very few words, tipped his head toward the pale and anxious Snow, and said, "Pleasure to meet ya, Snow." And then, with a look shot from Mam, he added, "Ah, and don't ya feel bad. There is *always* room at our table."

And with a few shoved seats and a game of Shift the Plates, they did make a space for Snow, sandwiched between Meghan and me. While we ate, I caught myself watching her out of the corner of my eye. As she talked to Meghan about girly shite I knew little about. As she discussed recipes with Mam and Kinsey. As she chatted with Granny about this and that. As she answered Sean and Patrick's prying questions. As she laughed along with Da's excruciatingly painful *dad jokes*.

There were these moments when she'd glance over at me, smile with those soft pink lips, and I'd find my knee bumping up against hers. I'd put my hand on her thigh, daring my fingers to move higher. I'd imagine those lips on mine, wrapped in her limbs in the cold cavern of my bedroom, and I'd look back to my plate of Christmas dinner and wish I was there. Without all of those yammering family members keeping us from more important tasks.

"So, how did ya meet?" Mam finally asked the million-dollar question with a wide grin. Her cheeks were rosy from her two glasses of wine, and her eyes twinkled with the hope that I had finally met someone worth being with. Someone complementary to my aesthetic and personality.

All I could think though, was how awful I must've been for this woman to not want to commit to me, even as she ate my mother's dry Christmas roast and over-boiled potatoes.

Snow took a sip of her water, her lips smiling against the glass. She looked up at me, and asked, "Do you want me to tell her?"

I cleared my throat and shrugged. "Ehm, well—"

"I'll tell her," she interrupted me, resting a hand on my arm, and my fist tightened around my fork. "So, I was heading to Canvas & Ink, and I accidentally walked into the vet clinic. Ryan here was sitting behind the desk, and I knew after just looking at him that I couldn't leave without at least knowing his name."

Her hand closed on my arm and my muscles tensed under her touch, hearing her tell the story as though it were an epic tale of boy-meets-girl. She kept out the dirty details of our fucking back at my place, and I saw the whimsical smiles spread across the faces of Mam and Kinsey. As though we were one of those cheesy, straight-to-TV movies they watched together on the weekends with a box of tissues between them.

"Women have never been able to resist the Kinney charm and good looks," Da said, pointing his fork at Mam. "Isn't that right, darlin'?"

Mam's rosy cheeks deepened in color. "Clearly, my husband has had a few too many t'night, but …" She smiled, inclining her head toward Snow. "There's really no denyin' it, is there? Kinsey can vouch for me."

My older brother wrapped his arm around his wife's shoulders, pulling her into him, and nodded. "I had her pinin' after me for twelve feckin' years before I got her to go out with me again."

Snow's eyes widened. "*Twelve years?*"

Patrick waved his hand in the air. "We had been together for a long time, we broke up, and she tried to resist—"

"How many times do we need to hear *this* story?" Granny quipped with a dramatic roll of her eyes.

"Seriously," Kinsey groaned, swatting at Patrick's chest. "And I still can't figure out what the hell I was thinking. I should have just settled down with someone in New York while I had the chance." She joked, rolling her eyes, but then she tilted her head against Paddy's shoulder, and smiled in the way she had always smiled with him. Like their souls were fused from the moment they were born and that was the only reason we were dragged as infants to the U.S. of A.

I wondered if anybody would ever smile like that when looking at me, when being with me, when just thinking about me.

I wondered if that could be Snow and I wondered if maybe it already was.

᪥

After dinner, as Snow gently played with Erin, I watched from the kitchen doorway. She rocked the little thing in her arms, cooing and grinning, and every so often, she'd turn to look at me. Delight was painted across her porcelain face, and I'd just toss her a half-smile while I still struggled to figure her out.

Patrick came up behind me with his all-knowing older-brotherly ways. "So, how long have ya been seein' her?"

Without Mam or Da around to berate me for the truth, I scratched the back of my head and my mouth upturned in a sheepish grin. "Ehm, four days now?"

He laughed through his nose, shaking his head. "Okay, let me guess … You took one look at her and conned her into goin' back to your place?"

"Believe it or not, it was the other way around," I said, crossing my arms and laughing with him.

"No shite?" He raised his brows and I confirmed with a nod. "I guess that shouldn't surprise me. Although I can't understand why she'd want *your* arse," he teased, and then nudged me in the ribs. "But you like her, right? I saw ya lookin' at her during dinner."

"Yeah, I think so." Oh God, I did, but I didn't want to say it so definitively. Not when she couldn't commit to me.

"Well, she certainly likes you," he said, leaning against the open doorframe, watching the strange woman fawn over his daughter like it were the most natural thing in the world.

"Ya think so?"

"Are you *blind*?" he laughed, smacking me on the back.

I considered that maybe I was. Figuratively, at least. Maybe I was so blinded by fear, by my past, that I was denying myself the privilege of seeing the way she looked at me from over there in the living room.

"She doesn't want to be together," I admitted, not knowing why. I heard the gentle melancholy in my tone, and I hung my head, scratched the back of my neck, and mentally berated myself for sounding like such a whiny bitch. Moping over a girl.

Patrick shrugged with a snort and a chuckle. "Dude, ya brought her over for Christmas, and she keeps lookin' at ya like *that*." He tipped his chin toward Snow with a smile as she looked up once again to grin at me. "If that's not bein' together, then I don't know what is."

৶

That night, after we had gotten back to the apartment, I helped Snow out of her dress and when she turned around, she caught my gaze and she smiled.

"I really like your family," she said lightly.

"They like you too," I said, watching the dress drop from her shoulders.

The flowing black material seemed to slide in slow motion off of her frame, pooling at her feet as she stepped toward me. Her hands were ice against my chest, and my skin was fire, my heart thumping against my ribs.

"I've, um … I've never done that before," she said, barely making herself heard above the whistling wind outside. Her hands slid up my chest and onto my shoulders. She stood on her toes, tipping her head back to look into my eyes.

"Done what?"

"Met a guy's family," she said, her fingers lacing behind my neck.

My brows knitted. "Never?"

Looking into her eyes, I could sense it; there was a part of her, somewhere in there, that wanted to let me in. To wrap myself around her and bring a permanent element of heat into that wintry world inside her gaze. I could feel the door opening, feel her teetering on the precipice, and then …

"I still haven't given you your Christmas present," she said, and before I had a chance to pull back and press further with my questions, she yanked me down. Took my mouth, snaked her pierced tongue along my lips before kissing me with an explosion of pent-up sexual frustration. "I've wanted you all fucking night," she breathed against me.

And any thought of prying further into her secrets floated out the open window as she broke the fevered kiss and lowered herself back to her heels, scratched her nails over my chest and stomach, and dropped to her knees. My hands were at the waistband of my jeans, but she pushed them away with a slow shake of her head.

"This is *my* present, and I'm going to open it myself, thank you very much," she teased, and her gaze never left mine as she pulled the zipper down with her teeth.

My heart jolted, and my breath hissed through my parted lips. "If that's your present, where's mine?"

"Patience, Ireland."

Her fingers wrapped themselves in the waistband of my jeans, of my briefs, and she pulled them to my ankles. And while I wanted to watch, wanted to keep my eyes on her and those feckin' soft lips, I was washed away with the warmth of her mouth and my eyes rolled, fluttered shut, and my hands found themselves tangled in the black nest of her hair.

She knew things. Knew when to use her lips, use her tongue, use her teeth. Knew just when to retreat, knew when to return. She knew when I was tipping over the edge, knew when to stop. Knew when to pull back, stand up, and shove me to the bed.

Her strength didn't allow her to knock me over; I fell willingly. Submitting.

It's what I had always wanted, always *needed*. It's what I could never admit to myself with anybody else; what male wants to feel powerless and out of control? Stripped of his masculinity, the very essence of what makes him a *man*?

But Snow wasn't anybody else. She took the power, allowed my submission where I needed it, without ever allowing me to feel like a lesser man.

Teamwork.

"You want your present?" she asked, turning around, giving me an excellent view of the tendrilled tree encompassing the greater part of her smooth back.

"Yes," I growled, watching as she coiled the sides of her black thong around her hands. Watching as she slowly bent over, putting on a show, sliding them over her legs.

Holding the scrap of fabric in her hands, Snow walked, naked and mouthwatering, to the head of the bed. She grabbed my hands from my pulsating groin, pulled them above my head, bound my wrists with her lacy underwear. She leaned over me, pressed her lips hard against mine, passing her tongue through my lips and teeth to lick my mouth just as another scrap of soft material was laid over my eyes.

"Merry Christmas Ryan," she whispered against my lips.

And the next thing I felt was her body encasing mine, pulling me blindly to the edge of the world, and I knew without a single doubt that it would only be a matter of time before I fell over.

I just hoped she'd be there to meet me at the bottom.

CHAPTER SEVEN
RESOLUTIONS & BELONGING

A week flew by, and I couldn't remember the last time I could say that, with the monotony of my life over the last two years.

Wake up. Go to work. Come home. Go to bed. Wake up and do it again.

Round and round, we go.

But that week, I had spent a portion of every day with Snow and I found that, as unconventional as it all was, I liked it. I liked sleeping with her, warming her forever frigid body with the fire of mine. I liked waking up to her, drinking coffee in the morning with her, showering with her, driving her to and from work on the back of my motorcycle, and seeing her on my lunchbreak.

A week and a half of that, and we had settled into a routine many couples don't find for months, or even years. But we weren't a couple, I kept reminding myself. She didn't want to be a cat. But there was honesty, and the freedom of simply being *together*. And I found that, at least for a while, that's all I really wanted. Hell, maybe even needed.

Teamwork.

And then, there was New Years' Eve.

§♥

We went to Patrick and Kinsey's place to celebrate.

They hadn't given the invitation with Snow as some sort of afterthought. There was none of that, "Hey Ryan, you should come over, and oh, you can bring that girl with ya, if you'd like" bullshite. Nah, Patrick had stopped by the clinic and said, "Hey Ry, you and Snow should come over for New Year's Eve. Tell her to bring that pie she made for Christmas. We haven't been able to stop thinking about it." I hadn't been able to control my smile when I accepted, because y'know, I had been in relationships with four girls, and none of them had ever been treated like *that*. Like they were really a part of it all.

And this was the shite I thought about while Snow sat on my lap on Patrick's couch, her arms wrapped tightly around my neck. She smiled at Sean, politely declining a glass of champagne, and he joked about there being that much more for him.

Kinsey laughed, pulling the bottle from his grasp, and said, "Oh no, pal. I don't think so. I pumped enough milk to keep Erin fed for the next few days. I'm getting drunk tonight, and that means this whole bottle is *mine*."

Patrick wrapped his arms around her waist from behind, kissed her neck. "That means these arseholes are leavin' early," he growled against her skin, and she pushed him off.

"I'm not letting you anywhere near me until Erin is at *least* four and the memory of childbirth is hopefully somewhere far, far, *far* away," and she turned, laughing her way into the kitchen.

Sean rolled his eyes, dropping down next to Snow and me, and inclined his head in our direction. "I don't know about you guys, but I'm leavin' early, whether he kicks us out or not. I don't wanna be around when those two start kissin' on the couch. Dealt with that enough when we were kids, but at least now I have my own place to run to."

Snow nudged him in the arm with an elbow. "Oh, come on. They're kinda cute."

"You wouldn't have thought so if you were the one gettin' kicked out of your own living room so the two of them could 'watch a movie,'" he grumbled, using air quotes.

I tightened my arms around her, tipped my lips to her ear and said in a growl, "And by that, he means, dirty ... hot ... sex."

Snow clapped a hand over her mouth, cheeks pinking as she laughed, and Patrick kicked his boot against mine. "Feck off, arsehole. Christ, are ya kiddin' me? We never had sex in the—"

"Patrick!" Kinsey hissed from behind him, and Snow bit her lip with a giggle, metal clicking against her teeth.

"What?" he asked, turning with arms outstretched. "These idiots think we would actually fuck on the couch in Mam and Da's house."

Kinsey looked around him, incredulous eyes staring at the three of us, and she shook her head. "Oh, hell no. Do you know what your parents would've done to me if they had found out?"

"Or walked in," Patrick said, crossing his arms and nodding. "Actually, nope. Wait," he held up a finger, "there was that one time when you were givin' me—"

"Are you at all capable of shutting up?" Kinsey asked, stepping toward him and smacking his chest, in sync with the lifting of her heels. "Fucking Irish bastard," she said, and he bent down to kiss her.

"And you love me," he said with a laugh, and I heard Snow swallow.

"Uh-huh," Kinsey groaned, as she smiled and clutched the bottle of champagne to her chest.

At midnight, Snow pressed her hands to either side of my face and pulled me to her. Her lips were on mine for a glorious five seconds, and then she hugged me and whispered in my ear, "I've never gotten a New Year's kiss before." The words wound through my ear canal, pushed into my pulsing veins, and slithered their delicious way straight to my heart.

"How is that possible?" I asked quietly, my voice graveled, my arms around her.

"Just enjoy the moment with me, Ireland." And I don't think I had any choice in the matter.

Kinsey and Patrick had occupied the recliner with a kiss that was heading straight toward that baby she swore she didn't want just yet, and Sean sat alone at the other end of the couch, staring at his hands and puffing his cheeks around an awkward sigh.

"Here we go," he muttered under his breath before taking a sip of his champagne.

Snow released me from her grasp, and she turned to him. "Hey, get over here," she beckoned him, and with a sigh and a small smile, he scooted over. Snow grabbed him by the chin and kissed his cheek, and said, "If *I* can get a kiss at midnight, everybody should."

Sean blushed, and my heart ... Goddamn, my heart pumped with enough life for three men, and not an ounce of disappointment.

Shortly after, when Kinsey started getting handsy in the recliner, Patrick really did kick us out, and that was just fine. Because the woman on my lap was toying with the hair at the back of my neck, reminding me that it had been approximately six hours since I had last had her frigid body under mine and I needed to warm her up.

And as we rode home, her arms wrapped around my waist, I couldn't help but enjoy the simple satisfaction of having the cold wind in my hair and my heart insisting on so many things my brain wished to be true.

&❧

The thing was, Snow had blended into us all like she was always meant to be there, and more than once, it had felt as though she'd grown up with the group of us. What scared me, was that I found myself wishing that she had. I wished she had shared in our childhood. I wished that I had known her longer, wished that I had met her before meeting all of those other girls. Before all the bad decisions, before the disappointments.

Before Cheryl.

Cheryl hadn't tried to get along with my brothers. Never tried to relax. Her presence with them was a stick up life's arse, a hindering chink in the chain, and I wondered, what the hell had made me think that was a good thing to hold onto?

And this was the shite I thought about as I buried my face into Snow's ebony hair and inhaled the scent of her herbal shampoo. As I wrapped my arm around her waist, pulled her into my body, content and satisfied. As I felt her smile in the dark, and I listened to her sigh.

"What are you thinking?" I asked her, my voice a whisper in the nighttime shroud that had fallen over my bedroom.

"I'm thinking that we should get a crockpot, and then we can throw dinner together before work. That way, we won't have to spend all that time cooking when we get home."

We.

Home.

Those little words that should have been by all accounts red flags, after only knowing her for a week, but … nah, my heart just pounded into her naked back, trying desperately to push itself beyond all of that skin and bone. To make itself at home in her chest, next to hers, where I suddenly felt was the only place I ever truly belonged.

I was so screwed.

Swallowing around the beating organ in my throat, I said, "*We*, huh?"

Her fingers interlaced with mine, pulling my hand between her breasts. "Yeah, *we*. You and me, Ireland. We need a crockpot."

I nodded, breathing in the scent of patchouli and exhaling the disappointment that had weighed me down for too long. *No more.* "Yeah, sure. We can grab one after work tomorrow."

"We can see if Sean's working and ask him to have dinner with us."

"Sure," I replied, burying my smile deeper into her hair. "I bet he'd like that."

"And we need to go grocery shopping, too. We're out of some stuff, and when we get a crockpot, I'll need shit to throw dinners together."

"You got it." My beard rasped against her skin as I kissed her shoulder.

Her cool back pressed against my warm chest, her arse wiggling against my cock, and had my thoughts not been somewhere far away, I would've grabbed her and buried myself in her again. But I didn't react to her obvious attempts at getting me hard, and she rolled over, putting us face to face.

"What are *you* thinking about?" She tugged at my beard.

"I think you should move in with me." The words tumbled out quicker than I wanted them to, but it was the truth. That's what I was thinking, that's what I wanted. I wanted it more than sex. So much more, and in the dark I could make out her smile.

"Now, what are *you* thinking?" I asked, pulling her into my chest.

"I'm thinking that's a relationship faux pas."

"We're not in one, remember?" I teased, sliding my hand down her back, along her spine where I knew the trunk of that tree was emblazoned to her skin. My fingertips grazed the curve of her perfect arse, my tongue licked the metal piercing through her lip, and I pulled her tighter against me.

"Why do you want me to move in?" Her fingers tangled into my hair. Her lips moved over mine.

I didn't hesitate. "Because I like having you around, and I feel like you belong here."

"Well, that's a first," she said, wrapping a leg around my hip. Pressing forward, taking me in. We sighed in unison, as though we hadn't just done this. As though we couldn't get enough. "I've never really belonged anywhere before."

I knew exactly what she meant, and I kissed her lower lip. "It's nice, isn't it?"

CHAPTER EIGHT
EX-GIRLFRIENDS & SKETCHBOOKS

And so, two weeks after Snow came to River Canyon, she moved out of her place over the Church Lady's garage and into my apartment in Granny's basement.

She was always here, anyway.

There were things she wanted, things she didn't ask for.

She wanted a TV, because she loved old movies. She wanted to use the other bedroom as an art studio. She wanted half of the bedroom closet, wanted a shelf in the bathroom medicine cabinet, wanted a different shower head.

She didn't ask for these things, but I gave them to her. Because I liked having her there, and I wanted her to be comfortable. I wanted her to feel at home with me, as much as I felt at home with her.

There was only one thing she *did* insist on: that I tell her the stories behind the cats. She said that, as long as she was living there, as long as she was partly responsible for scooping out the cat shite, she should know where their names originated from. I agreed that was fair, and so, one by one, the night she officially moved in, we went over them.

"This one?" She held up the Maine Coon.

"That's Jennifer—Jenny. She flirted like it was breathing, didn't care when I saw her doin' it either, and then I caught her fuckin' some guy at a bar."

"Oh, that's lovely," she said dryly, letting the cat scamper away to one of the cat towers in the living room.

"Yeah. I punched the arsehole in the face, sent him runnin', and all she had to say was, 'Calm down, Ryan. You didn't care when I slept with those other guys,' as if I had known about it." I told the abridged version of the story with my hands stuffed into the pockets of my jeans, walking around the apartment, unable to look at her.

She picked up the orange-and-black tabby. "Okay. Her?"

"Jessica, or, Jessie. While we were out somewhere, she had threatened to stab me when she caught me glance at another girl. I didn't think anything of it, until she really did stab me, when she thought I had flirted with Patrick's ex-wife." I pointed at a tattoo on my arm, and the raised line beneath it.

Snow looked startled at that. "Seriously?"

I nodded, eyes on the tattoo. "Yep."

"*Did* you flirt with her?" The crystalline eyes speared with anxious questioning.

"I would never," I swore, my voice unwavering. "Not only was she my *brother's* feckin' wife, but that's not what I do in general. But, still … Jessica saw what she wanted to see and attacked me."

The worry was gone, and she shook her head, disbelieving. "What the hell did she stab you with?"

"A can opener." I chuckled, running a hand over my hair. "Needed eight stitches."

"Jesus," she laughed uneasily. "You'll have to tell me the whole story someday." And then, she pointed at the black-and-white cat. "That one?"

Following her finger, I nodded slowly. "Tara. She was a more serious one. We actually lived together for a few months."

"So, you *have* lived with women before, aside from Granny and your mother," she teased.

"Yeah." I nodded, and for some unexplained reason, I felt the need to add, "And I'm pretty sure I loved her."

She thought I didn't notice that sharp intake of air, as she quirked a brow. "Only pretty sure?"

I shrugged. "I *was* sure *at the time*, but knowing what I know now, it might've only been the *idea* of her that I was really in love with."

"Deep," she nodded. "So, what happened?"

"Ah, well, I came home one day, and all my shite was gone. All my money, my TV, my laptop … Everything that was worth anything was gone, includin' her."

"Jesus Christ …"

I shrugged again. "I sure know how to pick 'em."

"Yeah, you weren't kidding. What does that say about me?"

"Not my girlfriend, remember?" I prodded with a gentle lift of my mouth, and she lowered her eyes to the floor. I picked up the white Persian, and sat on the couch, stroking her fur. She was my favorite. "This one, Cheryl, broke up with me, in a note."

"What did it say?"

I could feel that piece of paper between my fingers. Could still see those ugly words scrawled in her pretty handwriting: *"I can't continue to waste my time on a guy who would rather spend his money on silly things like tattoos and piercings. I can't waste my life on a guy who would rather sit with his nose glued to a sketchbook. You're not a man, Ryan; you're a* boy *pretending to be one. You're a disappointment, and the worst decision of my life."*

I tipped my head, mouth dry. "Ah, y'know," I cleared my throat, "I didn't take life seriously enough, I needed to grow up, I needed to stop spendin' money on stupid shite."

"That you were a disappointment?" I didn't have to answer that one; she knew, and her fists clenched at her sides. "That was the last girlfriend you had?" I nodded, and she shook her head. "So, your parents were never the ones to be disappointed in you?"

"No."

Finally understanding, she nodded once. "She broke you." I didn't respond. I didn't have to. She saw me, and she huffed angrily. "Ryan. You know that's bullshit, right?

The words in Cheryl's note had been double-stitched along my brain, and they had spoken loudly. But Snow's powerful presence in my life had dulled the voices, and I nodded once. "I'm workin' on it."

She held her head higher, satisfied. "What do you want to do with your life, Ireland?"

"What?"

She sat down next to me on the couch, petting the cat in time with my hand. "If you weren't working at the vet's, what would you be doing?"

I considered the question, and got up, putting Cheryl in Snow's lap. I walked over to a steam trunk that had belonged to my grandfather, opened it, and pulled out the first sketchbook on top. The trunk was full of them: all of my paperback secrets.

"What is this?" she asked, looking up to me after I had handed it over to her.

"What's it look like?" I smirked, a little more smug than intended.

She flipped back the weathered cover, and immediately gawked at the first scratch of black charcoal and pen. "You actually drew this?"

I nodded, sitting back down and kicking my feet onto the coffee table. "Yep."

She thumbed through the pages of black and white, her face expressing the awe I had expected, because that's how everybody looked.

"Jesus Christ, Ireland. You're so talented. Why haven't I ever seen you do this?"

I shrugged. "It's not something I do all the time. Just mostly when I'm bored, or angry, or upset, and well … With you bein' around, I haven't been much of any of those things."

Her pale skin did nothing to hide the flush of her cheeks. "I should teach you how to use a tattoo machine."

"That's actually something I've always wanted to do, y'know. Always loved tats, always loved drawing … Shite seems to go hand in hand, but then, you have the people you wanna impress, and they tell you that's not something to waste your life on."

She glared at me doubtfully. "Your parents?"

I shook my head. "Nah, they always encouraged me to do what I wanted, as long as I wasn't hurting myself or gettin' into trouble."

Her eyes darkened. "Cheryl?"

Reluctantly, I nodded, and she proved again to be as unpredictable as the weather when she stood up abruptly, pushing the cat from her lap, and began pacing the living room, clutching the book in her white-knuckled, black-inked hands.

"That fucking *bitch*," she growled, walking back and forth, each pass more heated than the last. "And you *actually* wanted to impress a fucking spineless whore like that?" I didn't answer right away, diverting my eyes, and she stopped in front of me. "Honestly, Ryan?"

"Yeah, I did," I said, looking up to her icy eyes, freezing me nearly to death. "She was the first *normal* woman to give me the time of day. She was a teacher, dressed professionally, didn't like spontaneity or kinky sex. She had her shite together. I mean, she had a feckin' *house*, Snow, and she paid her own feckin' bills. It was miraculous that she even gave me a second thought."

Her face fell, her anger crumbled. She knelt down, holding the book in her hands, placing it on the coffee table between us. "Oh, Ireland ... Fuck normal."

I smiled at my pet name. "Sometimes normal pays the bills, babe."

"Uh, this shit?" She touched the sketchbook. "*This* would pay your bills, and then some. A whole lot more than trimming nails and making appointments."

"I like workin' at the vet." Honestly, I did. I liked the animals, I liked the clientele ...

"But you *love* this," she said, picking up the book and pressing it to her chest. "And for what it's worth, *this* impresses *me*."

For what it's worth. My mouth slowly lifted one corner, then the other, because y'know what?

It was worth everything.

CHAPTER NINE
SHOWER HEADS & WINTER DANCES

The next day, my day off, Snow went to work, and I went out to Home Depot a couple towns over to buy the shower head that she said she liked.

Look at me. Romantic gestures and all.

But I wasn't a handy guy, and I had to call my big brother to come over and help me out during his lunch hour.

"You're sure about this?" he asked, holding the thing in place while I screwed it in.

"Sure about what?"

"Y'know ... *This*." He looked around the bathroom at all the girly shite cluttering the shelves and vanity. "Livin' with Snow."

"What do you mean?" I raised a brow at him, and he twisted his lips around something he knew I might want to punch him for.

"I just mean … after everything. You don't exactly have the greatest history with women, and it's a little, ehm … fast."

I twisted the screwdriver, glancing up at him. "This is different," I said, moving on to the next screw, pursing my lips and narrowing my eyes with concentration. "I like her. Granny does too."

"I do too. I think she's good for you. I just wanted to make sure you … ya know …"

"Thought it through?" I asked, laughing and stepping out of the shower, the new head successfully in place.

He shrugged a shoulder. "Yeah, well …" He nodded, resigning to the fact that I already knew what floated around in all of their heads. "Yeah."

I put the screwdriver back in his toolkit, ran my hands over the cool red metal, and shifted my jaw. "You don't think she's too crazy?" I asked, looking to him for his brotherly advice in the ways of love and romance. Lord knows he had that shite figured out from the earliest of ages.

And Patrick laughed. "Oh, I think she's absolutely insane, but she's your type of crazy, I think."

My type of crazy. I considered the idea that I could have a *type* of crazy, a *type* of *not quite there*. Those other girls, the ones before Cheryl, were they just my search to find the crazy that worked for me? Was Cheryl there just to prove that I couldn't *do* plain and boring? Maybe that's all any relationship was, I thought; finding a flavor of insanity to complement your own.

And maybe Snow was mine.

No … I *hoped.*

I *hoped* she was mine.

⁊❧

I woke up in the middle of the night to a warm bed, and that meant only one thing.

Snow was gone.

In an instant, I was out of bed and walking through the apartment, checking every room, every place she could have been. I contained my anger and panic with the security of knowing she wouldn't leave. But all I found was a group of cats, sleeping in different nooks and crannies, and no Snow.

I pulled on my sweatpants and ran up to Granny's part of the house. The door into the kitchen was always kept unlocked—*just in case*—and tip-toeing inside the dark and silent room, it didn't take long for me to know Snow wasn't there.

And so, I pushed my hands into my hair, closed my eyes, and pressed my forehead against the cool metal of Granny's refrigerator with concentrated breaths passing through my nostrils and out through my mouth. I had to calm down, I told myself. Her things were still there, her car was still outside. She wouldn't have left without her clothes, her shoes, her tattoo shite.

She wasn't Cheryl, and with that, my heart slowed to a calmer pace. I opened my eyes, turned my head to the kitchen window, and there she was.

She stood there, in the open backyard, with the blanket she brought wrapped around her body. Snowflakes sprinkled from above, scattering over her raven hair like stars against the night sky. I quietly opened Granny's backdoor, stepping into the cold, forgetting entirely that I was shirtless and barefoot.

"Snow," I said. Her name, not the change in the weather.

Her face was upturned, staring at the winter sky with eyes closed. Her black hair perfectly matched the gnarled tree branches, her skin perfectly matched the flakes falling from the sky.

She was spontaneity. She was unpredictability.

She was winter.

She was mine.

"What are you doing?" I asked, walking out into the blanketed yard, approaching with caution. Like she was some sort of wild animal, bound to run away if I dared make a sudden move.

But not Snow. She wouldn't run.

She opened her eyes then, turning to me. I saw underneath the blanket that she had at least the sense to put on her tank top and a pair of pants. Not that it did much to protect her from the cold, but at least she wasn't naked.

"It's snowing," she said with a little smile. Her voice barely a whisper against the muffled hush. She pulled the blanket tighter, clasping her hands against her chest. Her arms were tense with excitement, and her eyes sparkled.

The corner of my mouth lifted. "Yeah, I see that."

"I had gotten up to use the bathroom, and I saw the snow through the window, and I had to come out and see it." Her smile widened, and she took a step forward. "Will you dance with me, Ireland?"

I laughed, disturbing the silent night. "Get the hell out of here. It's feckin' freezin' out here."

"You should've put a shirt on, you idiot," she said, lifting the sides of the blanket to take me in. "Please, dance with me. It's snowing, and I've always wanted to dance in the snow."

"Where did you come from?" I narrowed my eyes at her, wrapping her in my arms, keeping her warm. It had never occurred to me that I should ask before that moment. Somehow it never mattered.

"Florida," she said, her arms tightening around me.

My features softened. "So … You've never seen snow before?"

"No. Well … not like this, anyway." She shook her head, her eyes lowering to my chest, as though she were embarrassed. "But I always knew it would be my favorite thing. It's beautiful, and dangerous, and unpredictable, and quiet."

Just like her.

"So, why didn't your parents name you, I don't know, Sunshine?" I chuckled at my own lame joke.

"I wasn't born with this name," she said, giggling a little as she glanced around at the world dressed in white. "I started calling myself Snow in high school, because it sounded bad-ass, but now … yeah. I can't imagine being called anything else."

I wondered if I should ask what name was on her birth certificate, but then again, did it even matter?

I sighed, tightening my arms around her. I rested my chin at the top of her head. "I'm a terrible dancer, ya know."

She pressed her face to my chest and smiled. "So am I."

But we danced, anyway.

And it wasn't much of one, to be fair. It was an awkward shuffle in the snow, a side-to-side type of thing with zero rhythm. Neither one of us was winning any awards anytime soon, and we wouldn't be auditioning for any reality TV shows, but whatever. I danced with her, because she wanted to, because she loved the snow. That was reason enough.

And even though I was shirtless and barefoot, even though the blanket had eventually fallen away to the ground, I found that I wasn't cold anymore, and neither was she.

CHAPTER TEN
PRODUCE & LABELS

"You really like oranges, huh?"

I watched as she pulled bags of the fruit from her reusable grocery bags, at least six of them in total. She grinned mischievously at me as she held up one finger, silently leaving the kitchen to bounce her way to the room she used as a studio. When she returned with a case in hand, she simply told me to sit at the table.

I decided to humor her and sat down without question.

"So, since you already have a job and wouldn't have much time to be our errand boy at the shop ... I don't think I could teach you there, *but* I figured ... I have all the shit we need, so why not practice here?"

"Practice what?"

She unfastened the case, opening to reveal the gleaming metal of a tattoo machine and its components. My eyes widened at the sight of it, and my bloodstream buzzed with excitement.

But then, I eyed her skeptically. "Babe, I don't think I have any skin left that I can reach, and I am *not* tattooing my own cock. I draw the line somewhere."

She laughed, tugging at my beard as she bent down to kiss me sweetly. "Don't be stupid. You're not tattooing yourself."

I glowered at her, shaking my head slowly. "No way in feckin' hell am I trustin' myself to do anything to your body."

"You do *something* to my body every day," she said, gripping my neck and kissing me again. Harder. And she couldn't just kiss me; she had to gently pull my lower lip between her teeth before setting me free.

The little tease.

"You know what I meant," I growled, suddenly desperate to do *something* to her body right then and there, among the fruit and tattoo machines. My fingers roamed her back, lower and lower until I settled over her arse. I groaned, flexing my hands, pulling her toward me.

"Nuh-uh, we're *working*."

"You started this," I pointed out, pressing my cheek to her breast.

"Later," she scolded, taking my hand from her arse, and dropping an orange into my palm.

"What the feck is this for?"

"Baby, this is what you're going to tattoo for the first time." She patted my shoulder before setting up the tattoo machine.

"Oh, boy. I've always wanted to ink a killer tribal dragon into feckin' produce. Dreams are comin' true here tonight." My voice dripped with sarcasm as I turned the orange over in my hand.

She rolled her eyes, unwinding a length of electrical cord. "I learned on pig skin, but I'm not buying any of that crap, so you're going to learn on fruit."

I groaned through the smile that tugged at my lips.

I was smiling a lot those days, a total contradiction of my life before. Before Snow.

I watched as she finished setting the supplies up, and I pretended to be annoyed when she told me she was letting me use her shitty machine. She didn't want me screwing up her good shite, she said, and I acted annoyed, swatting at her arse when she told me I was probably going to break it and buy her a new one.

I listened with excitement as she told me what to do. I felt that excitement bubble into eagerness as she showed me how to hold the machine. Hours upon hours of sitting through my own tattoos, and you'd think I'd know it all, but there was something different in holding the power between my own fingers.

"You have to learn how to work on a curved surface," she instructed.

"I can carve a mean pumpkin. You should see my jack-o-lanterns."

That old Kinney humor. It got us in trouble, and right then, it got me a light backhand to the chest. "Come on, this is serious right now," she giggled.

"Babe, this is fruit. There's nothin' serious about fruit."

She narrowed her icy eyes, and I held my hands up, surrendering to the very important task at hand.

"Okay, obviously this is a little different than flesh, but we'll get there. Right now, we're just going to work on pressure and learning how to work with a curved, textured surface."

And with her expert guidance, I pressed the machine to the dimpled surface of the unsuspecting orange. I willed my hand to steady, squinting my eyes with concentration and determination, and I watched those little needles jackhammer in and out, in and out, injecting the ink into its skin. That hypnotic hum soon lulled me to breathe steadily, my lip curled into a half smile, my tongue stuck between my teeth. Snow peered over my head, leaned against my back and worried her lip with nervous anticipation.

And after twenty minutes passed, I had inked the world's most incredible smiley face onto the side of an orange. Snow hung over my shoulder, resting the side of her head against mine. Temple to temple.

"Your first tattoo," she said adoringly, and turned to kiss my cheek before taking the orange from my hand. She walked away, holding it up into the light. "I can't wait to take this into the shop tomorrow, and tell Tre that *my*—"

She stopped herself from talking, stopped herself from moving. I turned in my chair, resting my elbows against my knees, watching her back. The slow movement of her shoulders as she breathed heavily, the slip of her tongue weighing heavily on her mind.

Maybe even on her heart?

God, I hoped so.

"What are ya thinkin'?" I gently pried.

She hesitated with a small shake of her head, black hair swaying over her shoulders, and I smirked at the back of her head.

"Hey Snow, talk to me."

She turned, clutching the orange in her hands, biting her lip tentatively. "I, um … I'm thinking I don't want to be a goddamn cat. I don't want you to go out and find some fucking black cat if we, uh …"

"Okay," I said, nodding. My heart hammered. God, it hammered so hard. "I can be a dog person."

"God, Ryan," she groaned, and she laid a hand over her eyes.

In the month and a half since she walked into the clinic, in the month since she moved in with me, I had learned very quickly that she only used my real name when she was serious about something. My name had never irritated or scared me so much as when she used it.

But right then, I felt hopeful.

"You won't be a cat, Snow," I insisted.

"Did you think any of them would turn into cats?" she asked, breathing heavily, pressing her hand to her eyes.

"No," I replied honestly, "but I also didn't have any of *this* with them. None of them were *you*, and that's how I know you won't ever be a cat. Or a dog. Or a feckin' gerbil. Nothing else could be *you*."

And she swallowed, hesitated, and then, her hand dropped from her eyes.

She nodded. "Okay."

"Okay, what?" I asked, lifting a side of my mouth into an apprehensive smile.

"I'll be your girlfriend. We can … go ahead and label this thing."

I laughed triumphantly, leaning back in the chair. "Why are ya okay with it now, but not before Christmas?"

She walked toward me, still gripping that orange between her hands. "Because, Ryan, you only wanted me to be your girlfriend when I wanted to meet your family. You wanted me to be your girlfriend, because we were having sex and you felt guilty about it. You felt like you had to, to avoid being some disappointment to some bitch that never mattered. But now? You want this, because it's what *you* truly want, and I want that, too."

Snow came to stand in front of me, and I reached out, pulling her between my thighs. I wrapped my arms around her, and I looked up to her face, my bearded chin between her breasts as she rolled the orange around in her hands. I stared into the chilly eyes of that strange feckin' woman, and I felt for the first time that I was looking beyond her exterior, beyond her eyes, and straight into the wild, calm, unpredictable core of everything that was Snow. I thought for a minute that I was looking at her soul, and it was comfortable and warm. Like coming in from the freezing cold, and I swore I felt the feeling of pins and needles pass through my fingers and toes as I thawed out.

A heavy breath passed between my lips. The rest of my self-doubt, self-loathing ... It left my body, left my lungs, and the air I breathed was clean. Fresh.

"You just fell in love with me." Her quiet voice pulled me from my world within her eyes, and I saw her face. Her soft pink lips, her white skin.

I cleared my throat. "How can you even know that?"

"Because I let you in."

"A little arrogant to think you have that kinda power, isn't it?" I asked, smirking.

"Yes," she agreed with a slight nod, "but isn't it the truth?"

And feckin' hell, it was.

My eyes held hers, delving deeper into that chaotic world of silent, snowy nights, as my hands slid up and under her tank top. The orange was placed lovingly onto the table, watching us with its unblinking eyes as the shirt was pulled up, over her breasts, and off of her arms. My mouth homed in on one nipple, drawing it between my teeth, rolling my tongue over the smooth round jewelry, as my hands went to work on getting her out of those pants. And I never once retreated from the world within her eyes.

"Don't fuck me here," she groaned, her lids drooping partially as my fingers slid easily between her legs. "I can't. Not when it's looking at me."

I released her nipple with a laugh and pulled her down to straddle my lap. "Come on, I've always wanted a smiling orange to watch me fuck my girlfriend."

But y'know, the truth of it was, I didn't particularly want to fuck her at all.

Because, in that world of icy warmth, there was no fucking. There was no screwing, or even sex. There was something deep and meaningful. Something binding. Something that said our crazy nipple-biting, back-scratching banging against the refrigerator door meant something more than just coming.

Hell, maybe it said *forever*, maybe it said *always*—I had no idea. But one thing I knew for sure was, it said that I loved that feckin' woman. I loved her more than drawing, more than cats. More than tattoos, more than cigarettes and motorcycles.

More than anything.

CHAPTER ELEVEN
L WORDS & CRUTCHES

Two months had passed since meeting Snow, and neither one of us had uttered the *L* word after that night when she saw what had combusted in my heart.

Initially, I didn't think it mattered. It was just a word, a word for a feeling that I knew we both felt in the purest, rawest of ways. I felt it in the way we constantly needed to touch; when we were throwing food into the crockpot, when she was teaching me how to tattoo the skin of dozens of oranges, and when we slept in our bed. I felt it in the way we talked to each other; the banter, the reassurances, the refreshing honesty.

The teamwork, the togetherness.

I felt it in the way we couldn't unlock our eyes when we made love, and Christ, when the feck had I started calling it *that*? It had all started as just sex—

fucking—but it had changed somewhere along the way, and we both knew it.

We just wouldn't say it.

And the thing was, the more we didn't say it, the more I thought about everything else that wasn't said. Why she had come to town, where she had come from, what had made her so cold. Those unspoken things, things that mattered when you loved someone.

I guess I was just realizing that I was desperately, hopelessly, in love with a near-stranger.

And I was getting sick of it.

&❧

I rolled off of her, undoing the seal of our frigid, hot passion, and she rolled back to me. Her leg curled around mine, pulling my thigh between her painted legs. My arm wrapped around her shoulders, one hand found her hair while the other found the growing length of mine.

"Christ," I groaned, spent and exhausted.

"Mm-hmm," she sighed happily, rolling a lazy finger over my nipple. "You know what? Tomorrow, I think I'll let you tattoo me."

"What? I've only been doing this shite for a couple weeks," I laughed.

"Yeah, but you're good. I don't think there's much more you're going to learn from fruit. You need skin, and it might as well be mine."

"You think I'm ready to ruin you forever?"

She laughed, pressing her lips to my chest. She held them there for one, two seconds. Imprinting herself onto my skin. "Oh, Ireland … you've already ruined me forever."

It was things like that. Those little things that weren't all that little at all, those little things that told me she loved me but just wouldn't say it.

I held in my sigh as I gently pushed her away from me, maneuvering to a seated position. Knees up, arms crossed over them. The window was open—it was *always* open—and I grabbed my pack of smokes and offered her one.

"Hey," she said immediately. "What's wrong?"

I shook my head, holding my lighter to her. "Nothing."

She pushed my hand away, holding the unlit cigarette between her fingers, and I lit my own with a shrug.

"Something's wrong." She grabbed my shoulder, and I shrugged her off.

"Tell me right now what you're thinking, Ryan, or I swear, I'll—"

My lips twisted. "You'll, what?"

"I'll leave."

It was cold, but, that was Snow. She was winter. Pleasant and cozy one second, cold and unmoving the next.

I sucked hard on the cigarette, shaking my head. "Nice, Snow," I said, choked with smoke, and I exhaled. "Really nice."

"Jesus, Ryan," she groaned, sighing through her aggravation. "You're being a pain in the ass, you know that? Just tell me what's wrong."

With the insult pinging at my nerves, I turned to her, resting my head on my forearms. "Why don't you talk to me?"

"*Talk* to you?" she parroted, her mouth open. "I talk to you all the time!"

"You do," I agreed, putting the cigarette to my lips, "but babe, you don't *tell me* a whole lot."

Her stare was blank. "I have no idea what you're talking about right now."

"Nah, I guess ya don't." The cigarette wobbled, flickering between my lips as I talked. The tension built, piling onto my shoulders. I didn't want to risk it, didn't want to push—not with her, and I wiped a hand over my brow, shaking my head. "Ya know what? Never mind. Just forget I said anything. It doesn't matter."

"No." She grabbed my hand, pulled it away from my forehead. "Explain what your problem is."

God, why had I said anything? I looked to her, looked into her eyes, and saw that the doors to my wintry world had shut, leaving me out in the cold.

I turned away and resisted the urge to shiver. I stared at the door—her escape.

She's going to leave. This is it. You're going to drive her away.

But I had come this far, and I plucked the cigarette from my mouth. "I've told ya everything about myself. You know about my past, the shite I've done, the women I've been with. I don't know shite about you Snow, and I can't shake the feelin' that you don't *want* me to know who you are."

I didn't watch the twisting of her lips, but I felt her grab the lighter from my hand. I saw her through my peripherals, holding the cigarette in her teeth, setting it to the flame, and then, she watched the fire flicker for a moment before letting it die.

I hoped that wasn't some sort of analogy.

Y'know … Little things that weren't all that little.

"There's nothing to tell," she said. Her voice flat, emotionless.

"Bullshite. Everybody has a story, and babe, you have one, whether you wanna tell me or not," I said, finally turning to her. My fingers pinched the smoke, hard. Harder, until it crushed under the pressure. "But that's bein' in a relationship with someone, Snow. You tell that person this shite. You should *want* to tell them—you should want to tell *me*."

Her hand robotically moved the cigarette to and from her mouth. The smoke fingered the air, swirling around the words that seemed so wise from a guy who barely had his own shite together. But the thing was,

I did have one thing together: my feelings for her. I felt better, knowing she carried the weight of my shame around with her. Knowing I wasn't alone. Knowing we were together, a *team*.

I had given her everything. I had changed everything. And she didn't have the sense—the *decency*—to truly share herself with me.

"Can I ask you somethin'?"

"What?" She wouldn't look at me. Her eyes were fixated on that feckin' door.

I wanted to nail it shut.

"Do you love me?"

She turned her head, slowly. "Oh, so is *this* why you're acting like a pussy?"

The jab curled my lips into a snarl. "I'm just askin'. It's not a difficult question. Pretty straight forward, actually."

"Why do you want to know?"

My mouth gaped, my cigarette hand drooped. "Why *wouldn't* I wanna know?"

"Because it's a *word*, Ryan. It doesn't mean anything."

I clapped a hand to my chest. "Maybe it means somethin' to *me*, or does *that* not matter to you?"

She didn't respond. Her nostrils flared, her lips pursing as a shaking hand brought the cigarette to her mouth.

"Snow," I said, warning her with her own name. "Why don't you talk to me? Why don't you tell me how you feel?"

Her gaze was pinned to the door. Her fingers wiggled, itching to leave.

It was coming. The storm of the century.

And I had forgotten to grab my coat.

"Because," she said, clambering off the bed with her back to me, "the second you start saying it, you stop *showing* it. The second you know me, the more you feel sorry for me, the more your feelings aren't real. Words are a *crutch*, *Ryan*, and I'm not going to lean on them. Not with this—not with *you*."

I stared at her back. The black branches that sprawled up to her neck, over her shoulders, with her skin highlighting the snowy drifts. The trunk that traveled the length of her spine. The trunk led to nowhere, just stopping in the middle of her back. Faded into the pale, blank flesh. God … I had seen that tree so many times, had flattened my hands over it, traced it with the tip of my tongue, but never had I grasped the analogy behind it. Never had I looked at it and *seen* that it had no stump to hold it in place, no roots to ground it—to ground *her*. Just a severed tree, with a severed heart, left to freeze in the middle of a wintry night.

"Jesus … What the hell happened to you, babe?" I struggled to keep my voice from quavering. To not speak in whispers, to not give away that I was terrified of her walking out that door.

She shook her head. "Nothing happened."

"Bullshite! Something happened Snow, and I'm askin' you to tell me what it is!"

She spun around, her face contorting with anger and sorrow, but something told me it wasn't necessarily directed at me.

If only she'd just tell me who.

I'd kill him.

"*Nothing* happened," she growled through her gritted teeth, her fists clenched at her sides.

"Jesus Christ, Snow! You are constantly goin' on, demandin' that I'm honest with you, and I have never lied to you *once*. Now, the second I need a real answer from you, you can't be honest with me? I want to feckin' *help* you!"

She grabbed the ashtray from her side of the bed, stamped out the butt angrily, and pulled her blanket from the foot of the bed. She scrambled to collect her clothes from the floor, and I asked what she was doing, where she was going. Anything to keep her from that door.

"Leave me alone."

The door opened. She walked from the bedroom, and I grabbed my sweatpants, pulling them on quickly before stalking after her.

"*No*, talk to me."

"You *really* need to leave me alone," she repeated, voice shaking and warning.

"I'll leave you alone when you tell me the tru—"

She shoved me hard. Pushed against my chest. I didn't move. I was too big, she was too small, but she shoved me nonetheless, and it was violent. It was rage.

"You will never, *ever* accuse me of lying to you, Ryan. *Never.*"

"Nah. I guess not," I said, a bitter undertone entwining through the words, weaving through each letter. "I guess ya actually have to talk to me to lie, right?"

I regretted that one immediately.

"Fuck *you*, Ryan," and she shoved again. Harder, and that time, I walked away, because now, I was the one who needed space. Now, I needed to be alone. I needed to breathe, I needed to smoke the rest of the cigarettes, I needed to draw something ugly and disgusting.

I slammed the door to our bedroom behind me, closing her off from me the way she had shut me outside of her. That wintry world I had made a home inside of, had locked me out, and I was freezing. I needed my anger to warm me up.

An hour went by, sitting on the bed, smoking and drawing. Charcoal smeared over the page, black tendrils sprawled against the white. The side of my hand was blackened with smudges before I looked up at the clock, and I noticed Cheryl, no—*Cee*.

All of the cats answered to different names now; Jessica was Jay, Jennifer was Fer, and Tara was Tee. It hadn't been jealousy that made her insist on that rule, but the desire to help me move on. She had simply pushed me to realize the past didn't matter.

She could have just shut me out, pushed me away, but she worked *with* me. She did things to make me the best version of myself, and not to *fix* me. Now, what the feck had I done when her moment came?

I fought her.

I drove her away.

"I'm a feckin' arsehole," I muttered to Cee. The cat slowly blinked her agreement, and I climbed off the bed.

The living room was empty. I wasn't surprised by that. The kitchen and her studio were also empty, the bathroom door was open, and she wasn't in there either. None of those things surprised me. I climbed the stairs to Granny's place, dark and quiet with sleep, and I looked out the window to see if she was in the backyard.

She wasn't. She wasn't anywhere, and *that* surprised me.

I walked quietly to the front of the house, looked out the window in Granny's darkened living room, and saw her car was gone. I ran down the stairs, my legs moving faster than I thought possible, and I looked throughout our apartment, and saw things had gone missing. The backpack she used as a purse, her coat, clothes from the laundry basket. Most of her stuff was still there, she hadn't taken everything, I told myself to keep the panic at bay, but then again, she didn't have much, did she?

And then, that's when the pain settled in. That dread that caused my throat to seize. I pushed my hands into my hair, squeezing my eyes shut, and I slid against the wall to the floor.

She had left, the one thing she knew to use against me. The thing she knew would hurt the most.

With my arms folded over my knees, forehead pressed to my wrists, I ran through every possible place she could be. I had never gone after a girlfriend before, but she wasn't like the rest. She was different, and I would find her. But before I could get dressed and on the back of my bike, there was a knock at the door.

I tripped over myself, standing and hurrying to answer the door, thinking it could have been her, but instead, I opened it up to find my older brother, looking as though he had just rolled out of bed.

"What the feck are you doing here?" I asked, and looked around him, up the stone steps leading to the backyard. Thinking that maybe, just maybe, he had found her and brought her home to me.

She wasn't there.

He sighed, pushing a hand through his hair. "I was gonna call, but Snow wanted me to come over and make sure you weren't freakin' out, but I guess you already got to it …"

"She's at your house?"

"Uh, are you gonna invite me in? I'm freezing my arse off out here." Grumbling an apology, I stepped to the side, and closed the door behind him. "*Thank you*. Anyway, yeah, she's at my place. She's stayin' there."

"Feckin' hell. For how long?"

Patrick shrugged wearily. "I don't know. A couple days, I guess."

"Wonderful," I grumbled, shaking my head. "That's just feckin' fantastic."

"Trust me, I'm not thrilled about it either, but Kinsey laid the guilt on, sayin' how Snow doesn't know anybody else around here, and—" He caught the look of disapproval on my face, the one that said for him to watch his tongue or I wasn't afraid of ripping it out for him, and he shook his head, resting a hand on my shoulder. "Nothin' against her, Ry. I'm just not thrilled about being woken up at eleven-thirty on a work night to your girlfriend cryin' on my porch."

"She was *crying*?"

"Yeah, apparently you really pissed her off. Can't say I'm surprised there," he said lightly, smiling.

Then he glanced at the table, noticing the two weeks' worth of rotten and tattooed fruit. His smile faded, and his eyes widened. "Ehm … What the feck are you weirdos doin' over here?"

"Snow's teachin' me to tattoo."

Patrick's mouth lifted into a grin, picking up one of the shriveled things. "That's pretty feckin' awesome."

I sniffed a laugh with a sad nod. "She was gonna let me do her tomorrow."

"I don't wanna know." He shook his head.

"She was gonna let me *tattoo* her," I clarified with a narrowing of my eyes.

"Ah, I gotcha." He nodded, putting the orange back on the table and wiping his hand on his pajama pants. "Jesus, she'd let you ruin her body forever? Chick's got it bad."

"Yeah, don't remind me."

"Okay, well," he sighed, "I have to get back home. I'm feckin' exhausted. But listen, Ryan: *don't call her*. She wants some space, okay? She said she'd talk to you when she's ready but leave it alone for now."

My mouth twisted in protest, shoving a hand through my hair, and Patrick shook his head.

"Don't do anything stupid, dude. She just wants some time, not a breakup, okay?"

I sighed, admitting defeat, and I nodded.

Patrick left, leaving me to sit in the apartment that was suddenly too cold, and too quiet. I closed the window and crawled into bed, terrified I would freeze right to death without that chilly woman laying with me, and I wondered if words really were worth that type of torment.

CHAPTER TWELVE
FIXING & FIGHTING

My parents had never met Jennifer the Cheater or Tara the Thief. They had known Jessica, for a short sprint of time, until she mauled me. But Cheryl …

Cheryl, they had known. Even with the awkward conversation and her snooty attitude, they loved her, because they thought she was *good for me*.

We had met at a tattoo place upstate, during a period of time when I was bouncing around from couch to couch, refusing to crawl home with my tail between my legs. She was there on a spur of the moment dare, trembling about getting a little rose on her ankle. I had watched the gorgeous blonde, completely out of my league, laughing with a friend, biting her perfectly manicured nails, all while I was having another piece added to my ribs …

"Hey, look at that guy right there, and you're afraid of a little thing on your ankle?" the friend chided, pointing at me.

"Does it hurt?" the blonde asked, hesitantly walking over to me with her hands wringing together.

"This? Feck yeah, it hurts," I laughed, and the gruff artist laughed with me, shaking his head. I knew the singular thought floating through his mind at the sight of the pretty little blonde:* poser.

"Oh, God, I can't do this!" she squealed anxiously, turning to her friend. Bouncing on her toes, shaking her hands.

I wondered what else she couldn't do; what I could convince her to do.

I smirked. "How 'bout this?" I said, grabbing her attention again. "You don't have to get inked if you'll go out with me."

Now, the thing about girls like that—the perfect bottle-blondes with their perky tits and shapely arses—is that they just *love* the *bad boy*. The cigarette-smoking, muscle-bound, inked-from-head-to-toe, motorcycle-driving bad boy that could make them feel *dangerous* and *daring* in their safe little worlds.

But the problem is, they can't love the *bad boy* forever. So, while they're fantasizing about the kinky sex, ropes, and whips, they're also thinking about everything they can do to fix that guy. A grown-up project to get another A+ on. Something to bring home to Mommy and Daddy, to pin on the refrigerator.

That's what Cheryl saw in me. But as for what I saw in her?

I saw hope. A chance at something better. A better life, something to be proud of, and Christ, I tried. I really tried, with a steady job at a vet's upstate and button-down shirts. But what happens when I try at something my heart's not in? I fail. I get distracted. I get fired. And so, Cheryl eventually got bored of the project that wasn't going anywhere, and she dumped me.

And this was the shite I thought about, sitting at my desk at the River Canyon Animal Clinic, while I missed Snow so much it hurt.

God, it had been four days since she started staying at Patrick's place. Four whole days. I had thought she'd be gone overnight, maybe two nights at most, but *four*? Kinsey had stopped by twice to grab some clothes, and both times, I asked her what the feck was going on, and when I could see her.

"Ryan, she's just thinking, okay?"

"How long does it take to think*?"*

I scrubbed a hand over my face and sighed, pulling a sketchbook from my desk drawer, fixing to throw my crazed thoughts down on the paper. Black and curled. Smeared and uncontrolled.

The door opened, the bell jingled, and I looked up to see Patrick in his uniform.

"Hey." I dropped my eyes back to the sketchbook.

"Hey," he replied, nodding and surveying the empty room. "Slow day?"

"Obviously," I grunted, the pen working.

"Right," he nodded, pushing a hand through his hair as he stepped toward the desk. "You're in a good mood, huh."

"Wow, nothin' gets past you." I rolled my eyes up from the sketchpad again to glare at him.

"What are ya workin'—"

I lowered my brows, scowling. "What do you want Paddy?"

He sighed. "Okay, look, Ryan. You have to get your girlfriend out of my house."

I chuckled. "Like I could actually get that woman to do anything."

"Can I give you a little bit of advice?" I gestured for him to get on with it. "I let Kinsey get away from me for ten feckin' *years*, Ry. I spent an entire *decade* of my life with a woman I couldn't stand, because I was too much of a little bitch to go after the woman I really wanted. Don't be an idiot and make the same mistake, okay?"

I dropped my sketchpad to the desk. "*She* walked out. *She* said *she* wanted space."

"Right. She did. But maybe *now* she's waiting for you to man up and go after *her*."

I thought about that for a moment, pursing my lips and shoving a hand through my hair. Manning up and chasing after her. Disregarding her explicit instructions. Fighting for her in a way I had never fought for a woman before.

I knew she'd be at work, and I stood up from the desk and walked to the door with sudden determination pushing me along.

"Where are you goin'?"

"I'm doin' what you told me to do," I said, my hands on the door.

"You're just gonna leave?" Patrick asked, spreading his arms wide. "What the feck am I supposed to do?"

"You're a feckin' cop. Watch the place for two minutes."

I hurried my way next door, immediately hit by the therapeutic hum of the tattoo machine doing its thing.

"Yo Ryan," the burly guy behind the desk said, offering a fist to bump.

To not seem too eager, I accepted. "Hey Tre. Snow around?" I asked as a courtesy, but I knew the answer. Two artists worked the place during the day. If the buzz wasn't coming from his machine, it was coming from hers.

"With a client, bro. She should be done in a little while, if you wanna come back later."

I worked my jaw from side-to-side, weighing out the options in front of me. I could storm back there like a tyrant, and demand that she talk to me right then and there. But that could get her fired, could get me in trouble with my own job for leaving the place unattended.

Christ, when did I get so responsible?

Yeah, I knew the right decision was to leave, and just wait. Walk away, talk to her when she was available, when *I* was available, but I had gotten this far, and I was done waiting.

"Yeah, ya know Tre, I don't wanna be a pain in the arse or anything, but can you just tell her I'm here? It's kinda important."

Tre heaved a sigh, rolling his lips around between his teeth. He weighed his own options, to disturb her or not, and I gave him a gentle nudge.

"C'mon, dude. I'll be fast. Just gotta tell her something."

He slowly nodded and moved from behind the desk. "Okay, but it's your ass if she gets pissed off," he grumbled, and I watched him head down the short and narrow hallway before he disappeared behind a curtain.

There were murmurs, his voice and a smaller one—Snow. I couldn't make out what she was saying, but the high-pitched edge to her tone suggested she wasn't thrilled with my surprise visit.

"Snow, just see what he wants, okay?" he said with a sigh, emerging from the curtain. He shot me a begrudging look as he sat down again. "She'll be out here in a minute."

"Thanks man," I said with a nod, and leaned against the wall.

I pictured Patrick, sitting behind the desk, manning the place while he was on duty, and yeah, I felt like a bit of an arse for abandoning him. But this was important, more important than some shitty job that I liked but didn't love.

Not like the way I loved her.

"Take a breather. I'll be right back."

Her voice floated down the hall, a whistle on a winter wind, and I closed my eyes, taking in the sound. *God*, I had missed her voice. Four days, and it had been a silent torture.

She walked down the hall and made her appearance in the waiting room. She peeled black latex gloves from her hands, snapping them away from each of her fingers. My eyes roamed her tank top, noted she wasn't wearing a bra, and my hands tensed into fists. She wore her tight black jeans, her combat boots that kicked my arse on a regular basis, and her hair was lifted off her neck into some kind of messy thing at the top of her head.

"Ryan." Her greeting was curt and cold.

"Snow," I said, mimicking her tone while wanting nothing more than to wrap her in my warmth and thaw her out.

"What's up?" she asked, crossing her arms over her chest, pushing her tits up.

I narrowed my eyes. Fixated on the outline of her nipple piercings. "Could ya maybe wear a bra to work?"

Snow shot a look behind her at Tre, sitting at the desk, and she turned back to me with mouth open and eyes wide. "*What the fuck, Ryan?*" she hissed. "You came here to tell me what I'm *allowed* to wear?"

I shrugged with a smirk. "It's just what I was thinkin'. Thought you'd like to know."

She huffed an annoyed sigh and grabbed her coat from a hook on the wall. "Outside. *Now.*"

I saluted Tre before heading outside. The wind whistled against my back, whipped my hair onto my forehead, and I squinted my eyes in defense of its brutal assault.

Christ, don't let that be a premonition.

"You have no right to storm into my place of business and tell me what to wear," she spewed immediately, fists hanging at her sides.

I maintained an indifference to my composure as I said, "Well, forgive me if I don't want people starin' at my girlfriend's tits."

"Okay, okay. Just stop." Her lids squeezed shut. "What do you want, Ryan?"

"I wanna talk."

She shook her head and groaned. "Did Patrick make you do this?"

"Yes." And then, I pinched my eyes shut, because goddamn her and the whole honesty thing. She had trained me so well. Maybe even too well. "I mean, I *wanted* to talk to you all along, but I also wanted to give you space. To cool off."

"Except you're forgetting that I know you don't talk, Ryan."

"All I've done is talk to you," I spat at her. "You're the one with the problem in that department."

"You know what I mean, Ryan. You don't talk when things are *broken*. You let girls leave, and then you buy a cat."

My eyes squinted at her. "So, Paddy was right. You were testing me, to see if I'd come to you." I shook my head, looking up to the sky. It was cool and gray. Snow was on the way, and I sighed with a sorrowful longing. For the weather, and for her. "I never *asked* to be left or kicked out, Snow. *They* left me without a feckin' *choice*. And I *promised* you would never be a cat, so you're not allowed to leave."

Snow pinched the bridge of her nose, sighing. She was giving in, I could sense it, and I allowed myself to feel a little triumphant. Hopeful, even. "Fine. Look, I'll talk to you tonight, okay? I have to get back to work. Come to your brother's house."

"No. *You're* gonna come home. You can't keep moochin' off of my family."

"*I'll* decide if I *come home*, Ryan. You come to your brother's house, and *I'll* be the one to decide where I go from there." Her lips twisted angrily, and I knew I was pressing my luck.

"Fine," I agreed reluctantly, because it was something, and I hesitated before turning on my heel.

Her lips were full and pink, and Christ, I knew they were soft and I wanted them. I wanted all of her, from her lips to the breasts I wished she'd cover up better, and all the way down to her toenails that I knew were painted black. Four days without having her was agony on every part of me, and from the taunting glimmer in her eyes, something told me she knew she was killing me. Something told me she loved it. And something in that turned me on even more, desperate to press her against the front of the building and have her there for the whole feckin' town to see.

But I didn't touch her, I didn't reach out and pull her into me. I kept my arms wrapped around myself and skulked back to the clinic, where Patrick sat at my desk, feet on its surface while he thumbed through the sketchbook.

"Have I ever told you what a talented arsehole you are?" he asked.

I quirked a brow. "Nope. Don't think I've heard that one from you before."

"Yeah, well, you are."

"Thanks," I said, almost moved by the unexpected compliment.

"So, you comin' by tonight?" He thumbed through a few more pages, grimacing as he went.

I nodded. "Yeah," I grumbled.

"Good," he said, standing up and dropping the sketchbook back onto the desk. "Because let me tell you … Ten years goes by fast, man, and you'll never stop kickin' yourself for all that wasted time. I know I never will."

CHAPTER THIRTEEN
MAKING UP & MAKING LOVE

The plan I had worked out in my head, involved a quick chat on my brother's porch, and then I'd throw her over my shoulder and drag her back to the apartment, where I could properly show her just how torturous four days without her really was. Maybe I'd say hello to my sister-in-law, a kiss on the cheek for my baby niece, but that would've been the extent of my visit at Patrick's humble abode.

Unfortunately, I hadn't calculated Meghan into the plan.

"Uncle Ryan!" she exclaimed the moment she let me into the house.

"Hey Meg," I said, breathless after she slammed herself against me in a hug. "I didn't know you were gonna be here. Where's your dad?"

Patrick appeared at her side. "Christine has an *appointment* tonight," he said with a hard glare.

"Huh?"

He sighed and leaned in closer. "She has a date," he whispered into my ear.

My eyes widened with surprise, and I nodded. "Well, okay then. Who's the lucky—"

Patrick shushed me, and Meghan rolled her big blue eyes. "Daddy, I *know* Mommy has a date," she said with an impatient sigh.

"Well, I didn't know if she wanted you to know," he replied. "You might've exploded with girly hormonal rage or somethin'."

"Ugh, Daddy …" Meghan groaned, throwing her head back. "You act like *you* didn't get married again, and I didn't freak out about *that*."

I laughed. "She's too smart for ya, man."

"Tell me about it," he grumbled before walking through to the kitchen.

Alone with my niece, I asked, "Ehm, Meg, where's Snow?"

She fiddled with the braid in her hair and said, "In the kitchen, making dinner with Kinsey. Are you staying?"

"I don't know, Meg. I have—" I began, but she wrapped her arms around my waist and looked up to me, her eyes pleading behind batting lashes. I couldn't say no to her, and so with a sigh and a grumble, I decided to stay.

"Yay!" She released me and clapped her hands before running toward the kitchen, and I followed with my hands stuffed in my pockets. I sauntered in, overselling my nonchalance, despite the booming of my heart smacking against my battered ribs. Snow was pulling the potatoes from the oven, bent over and assuming a position I could envision so vividly that I had to look away to keep myself from needing a quick trip to the bathroom.

She stood up, turned around with the tray in her hands, and her breath hitched with surprise. "Oh, hey."

I cleared my throat. "Hi."

Kinsey turned around from her work at the George Foreman Grill. "Hey Ry, you're staying for dinner?"

I nodded, glaring over at Meghan and her little grin. "Yeah, *someone* talked me into it," I muttered, and I watched Patrick give her a low-five. I shook my head, biting my lips to hinder the grin that couldn't be stopped.

Dinner commenced, where Patrick and Kinsey did a fine job of playing matchmaker, sitting Snow next to me at the table. It had been proven pointless though, as she pushed my hand off her knee anytime I made a grab at her. Digging at my pride a little more every time.

She was going to make sure I was sufficiently beaten and bruised before considering the possibility of taking me back, and that continued after the pork chops and roasted potatoes had been eaten.

We sat around the living room. On the floor, Meghan ooh'd and aah'd over Snow's tattoos in the way she would with mine; fresh material to ogle over. Kinsey sat in the recliner, tapping away on her tablet. Patrick sat on the couch, watching football recaps, and I sat next to him. Except, I watched Snow.

She held Erin in her lap, squeezing the baby girl with gentle affection. She talked to Meghan, gushing over TV shows and music groups I didn't even know she liked. She behaved as a friend one second, and like an adult the next. She smiled, she cooed, and she did it all so naturally and effortlessly. Not like some women, who had to push the motherly thing along like a boulder up a hill. And watching her, I felt something tugging inside me. Something uncomfortable and annoying, something waking up that had apparently been hibernating my entire feckin' life.

Christ, do I want kids? Do I want them with her?

And then, that's the shite I thought about, while I watched her.

Kids.

Mine—*ours*.

I wondered if they'd have blonde hair, like mine, or—*what color was her hair underneath all that black*? If their eyes would be an icy blue like hers, or something resembling denim like mine. If they'd be tall, short, or something in between. If they'd be angry, cold, hot, crazy …

My mind was pulled back to the real world when Patrick yelled something at the TV, and my eyes focused on Meghan holding Snow's arm in her hands, pointing at one small tattoo.

"So, when did you get this one?"

"Oh, wow … That was actually my first one *ever*," Snow said, looking fondly at the black ink on her left arm. "It's the pawprint of my first cat. I got it when I was just a little older than you. I begged my parents for weeks until they finally caved."

My eyebrows lifted. It was the first time she had ever mentioned parents, or any family at all, for that matter.

Meghan turned to her dad, who sat there with a look of disapproval plastered to his face. At the football game or at his daughter's conversation, I wasn't sure.

"Daddy! I want a tattoo for my birthday!"

"Yeah, good one, Meg."

"You had your lip pierced when you were my age!" she whined.

"And where did you hear that?"

"Kinsey told me."

"Traitor," Kinsey grumbled from the recliner.

I chuckled under my breath at how easily my niece threw her step-mother under the bus. "He had a mohawk too. Did she tell you that?" I threw in, and Meghan shot her shocked expression at me before shooting it back at her father.

"You said I couldn't dye my hair pink, and you had a freakin' *mohawk?*"

Patrick glared at me. "Okay, first of all, your hair is already red. That's close enough to pink, as far as I'm concerned. And second of all, watch your mouth around your sister." He gestured toward Erin.

"Daddy," she sighed impatiently. "*Freakin'* isn't even a bad word. Mommy lets me say it all the time."

Patrick returned her sigh with one of his own. "Yeah, well, when you're around your little sister, you keep the language to a G-level, got it? If they don't say it in a *Disney* movie, *you* don't say it."

"She can't even *talk!*" Meghan protested, her voice oozing with attitude and teenage hormones.

"Your uncle can tell you all about the stuff he didn't think he was teachin' *you* when you were around Erin's age," Patrick countered, throwing *me* under the bus, and I fought back with a smack against his arm. "Go ahead, Uncle Ryan. Tell your niece about the things she used to say."

I chuckled. "Ah, come on, Paddy. They're just words."

Meghan nodded enthusiastically, thrusting a hand toward me. "Yeah, *Daddy*. They're just *words.*"

"Meghan," Patrick said, his voice sounding an awful lot like our own father right before sending us to our rooms. "Enough."

The teenager threw her head back and groaned, rolling her eyes toward Snow. "You see what I deal with?"

"Hey, I've spent enough time with your dad to know he's a pretty cool guy," Snow said, shouldering my oldest niece and smiling. "Your whole family is pretty cool, actually, even if they don't let you get tattoos yet."

"Uh-huh," Meghan said with a roll of her eyes. "You're just saying that because you're dating Uncle Ryan. He's the only cool one."

Dating Uncle Ryan. Leave it to the kid to bring up the huge goddamn elephant in the room. That giant proverbial arsehole, sitting in the corner of the room, just waiting for someone to point him out.

"Yeah, well, don't tell your Uncle Ryan, but he's a pretty big loser."

Shocked, Meghan giggled, looking at me with those big, blue eyes. "Uncle Ryan is *not* a loser. Daddy is."

Patrick smacked the arm of the couch, turning to me. "Do ya hear this garbage?"

"You live in a house full of women, dude. Nothin' I can do to help ya. Have some boys. Build up your defenses."

Patrick glared at Kinsey across the room. "See? He agrees with me."

She looked up from her iPad, cocking her head. "Oh, that's great, babe. Then you can have a kid with your brother. Because let me tell you … Thirteen hours of labor isn't making me jump at the chance to have another one just yet."

Snow giggled so girlishly I wanted to poke fun at her, had I felt I held the right to. She clapped her hand over her mouth and turned back to me, truly acknowledging me for the first time all night. "I hope you'll be *very* happy together," she said through her fluttering laughter. "I guess Patrick will be wearing the pants in that relationship?"

"Oh yeah? Come here and say that," I growled at her, my eyes darkening with the reminder that I hadn't gotten laid in four days. The things I would do if she just got a little closer.

"What are you going to do to me if I do?" she asked, trapping her lower lip between her teeth. Proving to me that her desire was still there, even if it was buried under five inches of ice.

Clutching the arm of the couch, I tipped my chin, glared at her through my lashes with carnal intent, and just as I opened my mouth to speak, Patrick's voice collided with the dirty thoughts flooding my mind.

"Well! Meghan, you have school tomorrow, and you need to get in the shower before bed. Kins, I'll grab Erin, and you get her pajamas together, okay?"

Kinsey jumped up from the recliner, eyeballing me with a warning glare. "You better behave yourself. I don't want to have to douse my couch with gasoline tomorrow, got it?"

"What?" Meghan asked, looking between Kinsey and me.

"Don't worry about it," Patrick said, nudging her gently with his foot. "Upstairs. Bed. Now."

I drowned out the Father-Daughter banter as my brother scooped Erin up from Snow's lap and pushed Meghan along toward the stairs. I ignored their footsteps heading up, ignored the closing doors and whining teenaged voice echoing down to the first floor. Because I was sitting there, looking into her crystal eyes, begging her to open up and let me back into my chilly world.

"You're good with kids," I said to her, nodding with sincerity.

Looking embarrassed, almost a little sad, she said, "I always wanted them."

"You still could."

"Oh, yeah, I'd make a *great* mother," she laughed, but she was moved by the comment. She had dropped her gaze, picked at the hem of her tank top.

"I think ya would."

"Stop it Ryan. Please."

I sighed, deflated. I touched her blanket, folded on the back of the couch. She had been sleeping there for the past four days, letting it collect her scent while it faded from our bed. I felt stupidly jealous of the damn thing, that feckin' couch. Getting her all to itself.

Who the hell gets jealous of a couch?

We fell into silence for too many minutes. I was afraid to speak, afraid to move. Afraid to do the wrong thing, afraid to leave. So, I sat there, touching her blanket. She sat there on the floor, finding something interesting in the carpet, until finally ...

"Ryan," she finally said, bringing my attention back to her.

"Yeah?" I rasped and cleared my throat.

"I, um ... I'm sorry I left the other night. I know how much that freaks you out, and I shouldn't have done it. It was such a bitchy thing to do."

I chewed the inside of my cheek as I shrugged. "It's okay."

"No, it's not," she said, finally looking back up to me. Her apology searing through her glassy eyes.

"Okay," I said, submitting. "Why did you do it, then?"

She sighed, pulling her knees to her chest. "Because I knew it would fuck with your emotions, and I wanted to scare you. I wanted to control you, the way you tried to control me."

"I'm not—"

She shook her head, holding a hand up in front of her face. "You're lying to me. You wanted me to talk to you. You *demanded* it."

"It's not askin' a lot to want my girlfriend to talk to me," I countered.

"No, it's not, but Ryan, did you ever think that maybe I was waiting until I was ready to talk?" She shook her head, strands of black falling against her cheeks. God, how badly I wanted to just tuck them behind her ear.

"You could have just said that."

"You wouldn't let me," she stressed. "And then, there was all that love crap, and—" She sighed, pushing her hands into the mess of her black hair. "You can't make me say things I'm not ready to say. You can't just snap your fingers and demand that I do things when you want me to do them. It doesn't work that way."

I listened to her. I took in her words, and I sighed, nodding. "Then, I'm sorry too."

"Thank you," she said, mustering a hint of a smile.

"We're both pretty messed up, huh."

She nodded slowly. "That's kinda who we are, I guess."

Who we are.

A big feckin' mess.

She sighed, chipping the polish away from her nails. "But, I think I'm ready to talk. If you wanted to listen."

I looked down to my lap, to my hands, and I smiled.

Yeah, we were a big feckin' mess. Unorganized noise. But together, Snow and me ... Our mess, our noise ... It was music, and it was ours. And I felt the faintest of winds blowing me back into my little wintry world of warmth and ice.

"What are you thinking?" she asked, hushed against the ticking of a clock coming from somewhere in the house.

I looked over to her, found the hopeful smile gracing her soft pink lips. "Well, I'm thinkin' I desperately wanna know your story, but first, I wanna take you home, because I'm fairly certain my brother would literally murder me if I made love to you on his couch."

"Oh *God*," she groaned gutturally. "Don't *ever* say that again, *please*."

"What?" I laughed.

"You know *what*. We don't do *that*. I might love you, but we don't do *that*."

I grabbed her hand, pulling her to her feet. She stood between my spread legs, and I wrapped my arms around her waist. "So, wait a minute … You *might* love me?"

"Don't push your luck, Ireland. I'm taking you home, we'll pick up your bike tomorrow."

"My name's Ireland. By nature, I'm pretty feckin' lucky," I teased, pressing my ear to her chest, listening to her heartbeat, and all I could think about was that word …

Home.

And I knew, from that point on, she was *mine*.

CHAPTER FOURTEEN
LONG TALKS & LAME SHITE

"Good God," she breathed, kissing me as she untied my wrists from the headboard. "For such an old man, you sure have a lot of stamina."

"Four days of nothin' will do that," I laughed, and passed her a smoke. My brow crumpled. "Wait a minute ... *Old man*?"

She laughed, taking the cigarette from me. "Old compared to me."

"I'm thirty!" I barked with a laugh. "Why? How old are you?"

"Twenty-nine," she said with a giggle, and I rolled my eyes. "Well, you *are* older than me."

"Hardly," I grumbled, but I smiled. "Do you think it's crazy we don't know much about each other?"

She shrugged, tapping the end of her cigarette against my chest. "It might be, but maybe it's just us—our thing. And hey, we'll learn as we go along, right?"

Our thing. Our type of crazy.

My smile broadened as I lit her smoke then lit mine. I stared at the ceiling as my arm curled around her shoulders. This was my favorite place in the entire world: lying there with her, sending our smoke streams swirling together into the chilled open-window air.

Christ, I loved the feckin' cold. Always had but being in love with winter certainly helped. You grow accustomed to the feeling of your fingers and toes always being cold, while your heart soars with the heat of a cracking fireplace.

"Ask me." She tapped on my chest.

"Ask you what?"

"You know."

I smiled. "Okay, okay ... What are you thinkin'?"

"I'm thinking I'm ready to tell you what happened to me," she said, releasing a tense breath of air.

"I thought you said nothin' happened to you," I teased, brushing my fingertips over her ear and neck.

Snow sighed, gently pulling from my grasp to sit beside me. "I wasn't kidding. It was really *nothing*. Just ... a nothing relationship that went absolutely nowhere."

I pointed my cigarette at her. "I *knew* it *was* a guy. It's always a broken heart that screws us up the most," and she nodded her agreement solemnly. "But it's always someone else that helps us to fix it, too," I added, and she bit the inside of her cheek.

And so, she talked, the cigarette waving in the air as she spoke animatedly with her hands. "There was this guy … *Dave*." She said his name with disdain, and I felt every bone in my body, one by one, tense at knowing who the arsehole was. "I met him at a bank I worked at in Florida."

I scoffed. I didn't intend to, but I did. "*You* worked at a *bank*?"

She pointed her cigarette fingers at me. "Hey, you're a fucking *secretary*," she teased with the slightest hint of a smile before she tapped back into her fractured heart. "*Yes*, I worked at a bank, and I didn't *like* it, but I had gotten into some shit when I was younger. Did a *lot* of drinking, some recreational drugs, got into some trouble with the cops. Nothing too serious, but I was heading in the wrong direction. And the crappiest thing? I did most of it, because I was trying to impress some guy, or some friends." She laughed at herself, shaking her head, and I plunged into the crystal lake within her eyes.

"It happens," I said, interrupting her again. "Most of the stupid shite I did only happened because my friends were doing it. Or because I wanted them to like me more. Lookin' back, I wish I had spent more of my energy on my family. Ya know, people that actually matter."

Snow smiled, touched her hand to my face. "But they never stopped caring."

My eyes squinted at her. "Your parents ..."

She took a deep breath of preparation. "They had an interesting way of showing they cared. Honestly, I think it's more that they just didn't know what to do with me. I was out of control, they were at their wits end, so they told me I had to get my shit together or else they'd kick me out."

My face turned to stone, my fist clenched. "They were going to *give up* on you?"

She hung her head. "I don't know if it was so much a matter of giving up, or if it was just that their way of helping was to scare me, and anyway, it worked. I didn't particularly want to be homeless, so I got a job as a bank teller, and it sucked ass. But, it was a steady, decent paying job. And I mean, in a lot of ways, it *was* a good thing. It kept me busy."

She took a long drag from the cigarette, looking up to the open window like she wanted to be out there. Like being there, in that room, was suffocating her. I took a glance in the direction she looked, and saw the drifting of snowflakes, illuminated like twinkle lights from the gentle glow of the outside world, and in a moment of spontaneity, I jumped out of bed.

"What are you doing? I'm still talking."

"Yeah, I know. I'm sorry," I said, pulling on my sweatpants and then my boots. "But you can talk outside. Come on."

With a forlorn sigh and an affectionate smile, she nodded, and got dressed. I threw on a sweatshirt, grabbed her blanket and a couple of pillows. We climbed the stairs to the snowy backyard, and I made a bed out on the lawn and laid down.

Her crystalline eyes twinkled with tears I hoped wouldn't fall. "When did you get so lame, Ireland? Did I do this shit to you?"

I glared at her. "Shut up and get down here with me."

She sighed, her breath sending a silvery cloud into the air around her face, and she sat down, lying herself back into the crook of my open arm. I pulled the blanket around us, forming a cocoon. Two unconventional people, trying to sprout their wings in a world of people wanting them to change.

Feck the world.

I kissed her hair, inhaling that herbal scent. "Okay. Continue."

Through my sweatshirt, I felt her smile against my chest, and her arm tightened around me, absorbing my heat into her forever chilly body. She wouldn't admit it, but she loved that lame shite, and ya know what? So did I.

"Okay. So, Dave ... Every week, this guy would come into the bank to make his deposits. He noticed me before I noticed him, and he started waiting to make sure he had me as his teller."

As I listened, I blinked at the snowflakes falling into my eyes, fantasizing about what this Dave arsehole could possibly look like. Better looking than me? Bigger than me?

"The other girls at the bank thought it was weird. Kinda obsessive, you know? And I guess it probably was. I mean, looking back, it was actually really creepy. I was a twenty-year-old, being pursued by a man easily ten years older than me. But, at the time, I thought it was sweet, because this guy really had his shit together. Like your Cheryl. He wore expensive suits all the time, and he looked damn good in them. He *smelled* rich, brought in big checks, drove a fancy car, and it felt *good*. You know … To be attractive to someone like that."

My Cheryl? "Cheryl's not mine," I said, my voice feeling weighted in my throat.

"She *was*." She reached a hand up, touching my lips with her fingers. I kissed her fingertips.

"So, this went on for a few months, and every time, he'd get a little braver. Complimenting me a little more, asking me questions, and then finally, this one time, he saw my tattoos under the sleeve of my shirt. He got bold, grabbed my arm, and pushed my sleeve up a little bit, and *God*, it turned me on so much. Like … like I was given an invitation into this world I clearly didn't belong in, you know?"

I swallowed the vile taste that had collected in my mouth at the mention of her being *turned on* by some other arsehole, and I nodded, because I did know.

"Anyway, he asked me out that same day. He wanted to take me to this *amazing* restaurant that cost a fucking fortune, and I said yes. And … ugh, Ryan, it was like, like …"

"Livin' another life?" I offered.

"Yeah," she said, the word clinging to a sigh. "I mean, I'm not one to follow stereotypes or whatever, but I think if I had been there with someone else, it would've felt weird—like you, no offense."

"None taken," I said, and I choked around a stiff chuckle.

"But being there with him, I felt like I stuck out like a sore thumb, but … I also felt like I belonged there, because he was there in his expensive suit. Does that make sense?"

I shrugged. "Cheryl's parents took us out once to this seafood place that charged about a hundred bucks for a lobster, and I felt like a feckin' child when she insisted on dressing me and doing my hair. She ran me through a crash course on how to behave, what to say, what to do ... until she told me to just not say anything at all. Her yuppie parents were grateful," I laughed, and I winked at her. "I never really *belonged* there."

"God, what a bitch," Snow laughed.

I nodded, because goddammit, she really had been.

"Anyway … Dave and I went out a few more times after that. He liked to impress me with his money, so he'd spend a lot whenever we did anything. Expensive concerts, expensive dinners … And then, after one of those *dates*, he took me to the fanciest hotel I had ever been to, and we …" She hesitated, breathing into my chest. "God, I don't know if I can talk to you about this."

"It's okay," I said, squeezing her tightly against me, reassuring her. Wishing someone were there to reassure me.

She sucked the frigid air into her lungs. "We slept together that night, and I hated that it wasn't this *huge deal* for him, because it was for me."

"But sex with me was nothing?" I chuckled, not caring a bit about how jealous I sounded.

"It wasn't *nothing*," she said, wrapping her arm tighter around me, and she added, "But I also wasn't a virgin with you."

We were laying out in the open air, under a snowy sky, but a bubble formed around us. A stifling encasement void of oxygen.

"So, he was the first guy you had ever been with," I stated unnecessarily, and she nodded against me.

"Yes," she said, speaking the word as though it hurt. "I was one of those lame bitches who thought I was better for saving it for someone who mattered."

"That's not lame Snow."

"Yeah, well, maybe you don't think so, but a lot of people did. And still, I saved myself for someone *special*," she snickered, and something told me he hadn't been all that special at all.

"It's actually funny, because my parents had always pushed that on me—*sex is special*—you know, that whole spiel, and I took it to heart. I gave myself to someone I *thought* would be it for me, and he turned out to be … well, I'll get to that, but when I came up here for a fresh start, I saw you and thought, 'I'm going to have the most amazing, meaningless sex with that guy.'" She laughed, choked by the uprising of emotion. "*God* … how's that for ironic?"

I held her closer to me. "Yeah, and I thought *you* would be the mistake," I said and kissed the top of her head. "Go on. Tell me the rest."

"Okay, so … Our relationship, or whatever it was, continued for a few more months. I fell in love with him, and he said he loved me. Things felt so right between us, and my parents were fucking thrilled that I found him. Oh my God, they *loved* him. They—"

"Wait, how old was this guy?" I asked, eyes narrowed at the sky.

"Thirty-three."

"And you were twenty, you said?" She nodded against me. "So, your parents were thrilled with a thirty-three-year-old man pursuing their twenty-year-old daughter?" I asked through my skepticism. I was having visions of an older silver-tongued devil putting the moves on a girl only six years older than Meghan. I couldn't imagine my brother taking that shite without permanently implanting his boot up the guy's arse.

Snow shifted uncomfortably against me. "Um … well, they didn't know how old he was, and they never *actually* met him. Plans never panned out—"

"Big surprise there," I grumbled. My throat tightened around the protective wish to have known her then, to have been able to ring my hands around his neck before he had the chance to dig his fingers into her.

"Yeah," she said, and I felt her shame. "I'd tell them about him though, and they'd talk about what a blessing that bank job was, and for a long time, I believed that too. Because for once, everything felt so … *together*, at least in my mind, and I could actually see myself getting married, having a couple of kids … You know, having a life I didn't actually picture myself ever having, with a man I could never in a million years imagine being with.

"But then, he disappeared for a couple weeks. I couldn't get a hold of him, his cell phone was turned off, and it dawned on me that I didn't even know where he lived. I tried looking him up, but do you know how many David Fords there are?"

She gripped my sweatshirt, as though trying to pull from me the strength to continue. "God, I should have been freaked out, right? I mean, looking back, that's some scary shit! For someone to just … drop off the face of the fucking planet like that. But … I was so in love, and I was so *stupid*, Ryan, and I was so happy when he finally called me. For two weeks, I didn't hear a fucking thing from him, so I asked where he had gone, what had happened, and I told him how worried I had been. I expected him to tell me that something terrible had happened to him, and I almost wished that's what it was, because you know what he told me?"

"Married." My mouth was dry, and my throat hurt to swallow that heavy load of anger and disgust.

She lifted onto an elbow and looked down at me. "How could *you* know that, but I couldn't see it when I was the one *with* him?"

I smiled weakly, shaken by the ache in my chest. "Because you were sleepin' with him babe, and you loved him. That shite will make you blind to anything."

She lowered herself back down, looking up at the snow sprinkled sky. She laughed lightly, the sound disappearing into the night. "Yeah, well, not only was he married but he had three kids. He had been on vacation with them, he said. He acted like it was the most normal thing in the world to be in fucking Vermont, skiing with his family, while his *mistress* worried about him for two weeks.

"I was so upset, that I could be so stupid. That he could be that person. I mean, you hear about that shit happening to other people, but you never think it can happen to you, you know? You never, ever think you could be the *other woman*, and I was so disgusted with him. I was so, *so* fucking *sick* to my stomach over it, but surprise-surprise … He said he was so in love with me, he only wanted to be with me, he was going to leave her, and goddammit, I fucking believed him. I believed him for *so* fucking long, Ryan, and I fucking hated myself for it, but I loved him."

"How long?"

She turned her face into my chest, and uttered a muffled, "Seven years."

"Jesus Christ, Snow," I said, hushed, with a shake of my head.

"Oh, it gets better," she said, her voice catching in her throat.

Christ, she was going to cry.

If she cried, I knew I would break.

She sighed, sucking in a quivering breath. "A couple years ago, I thought I was pregnant. And I was actually happy, because I thought that would be the thing to do it. Like, *that* would be the thing, to finally make him leave his wife, to finally be with me completely, and I'd be able to see him or call him whenever I wanted without worrying if she'd catch us."

"Holy feckin' shite," I grumbled, pinching my eyes shut. "Seven years, and she never knew?"

Snow sniffled and shook her head. "Nope. I hated her for a long time, but then, I was kind of jealous of her. Like, she was clueless, living in this oblivious little bubble with her rich husband and kids. She had no idea I was in the picture, but I knew about her. I knew about all of it, and it hung over me, like this constant reminder of what she got to first."

The tears broke through, falling against my sweatshirt. She turned her face, hiding herself and her pain, and I gripped her shoulder.

"What happened?" I asked, urging her to continue.

She breathed through the tears and the pain, wiping a hand over her face. "Um, well, I told him my period was late over dinner. And I waited for him to be happy. I sat there, all excited in this ugly pink dress I wore because *he* liked it. I was grinning like an idiot for—God, it had to have been minutes before I realized he wasn't happy. He just kept staring at me with this *look* on his face, and he said ..." The sob bubbled up, her fingers gripping hard against my sweatshirt. "H-he said, 'If you're knocked up, you better get rid of that fucking thing. I can't have my whore walking around, pregnant with my kid.'"

My jaw trembled, my teeth chattered, and it had absolutely nothing to do with the cold.

I was hot with rage, and I wondered, how quickly could I get to Florida? How long would it take for me to get down there, find the son of a bitch, and watch the life fade from his piece of shit eyes as I choked him?

My fist clenched, my breath came in tight gasps, and Snow lifted onto her elbow again.

"Ryan." Her bitter cold hands pressed to my cheeks, chilling my heated blood.

"I'd kill him, you know."

She smiled, leaning down to kiss me with her tears falling against my face, and nodded. "I know."

I took a deep, controlled breath, finding my calm in the wintry world beyond her eyes, deep within her soul. "Okay," I said. "What did you do to the piece of shite?"

She tapped my chest, keeping her eyes on my face. "Well, when he called me his *whore*, I did the natural thing and slapped him across the face."

Swelling with pride, I laughed. "I hear it's okay to stab someone too."

"Yeah, well, if I had known about that, I would've grabbed my fork and stuck it in his dick, but you know … Can't live with regrets," and she giggled, her tears drying.

"Hey, it's not too late. Ya think I could take him?"

"He'd shit his pants if you came after him," she laughed, dropping her forehead to my shoulder. "You know, it might be worth it, just to watch him ruin one of his expensive suits."

I was bigger, stronger, tougher.

But I didn't need to know that to know I was, for once, the better man.

"Were you pregnant?" My stomach felt hollow and cold as I asked the question, but I needed to know.

She lifted her head again. "A couple of days after I left him, I got my period. It was so stupid too, because I still kind of wanted it. Like, even if I couldn't have him, I'd still have a part of him."

I touched her face, running my thumb over her cheek. "That's not stupid, babe."

She looked in my eyes, and smiled, pulling me in further. Leading me back to the fire I had built in my little wintry world, surrounded by ice and my Snow.

Without saying another word, she shifted under the blanket, lifting a leg over to straddle my waist. I hardened instantly, nestled at home between her legs. She leaned forward, pressing her lips to mine, stringing little kisses together until her tongue joined in the fun, licking across my bottom lip. Coaxing my mouth open with little resistance, and she moaned.

"Wait, wait," I said into her mouth.

"Come on Ireland. It's snowing, and I want to fuck you," she whined, and made an attempt to shove her tongue back into my mouth.

I laughed, pushing her away gently. "I just want to know something first."

"You are *really* taking advantage of this honesty thing."

"Why did you leave Florida? Did you run away from him? Were you afraid?"

She laughed, dipping her head to my neck, the metal stud on her tongue chilling a trail from my ear to the collar of my sweatshirt. I closed my eyes, tipping my head against the pillow with a low, primal growl.

"I left two years after all that happened. He had nothing to do with it," she said against my neck, her voice tickling against my skin.

"Then, why?"

"Ugh, Ryan ..." She sighed impatiently.

"You know everything about me. You know about the cats, my past, the fact that my parents handle my feckin' bills—"

"—yeah, we need to work on that one—"

"You know about the shite I'm scared of, my insecurities, and everything else that nobody else knows about. I am so feckin' in love with you to the point that I am willin' to fly down to Florida and strangle the life out of some guy just for callin' you a whore. And, I have no idea why—"

She pushed herself up against my chest, sitting abruptly, and the places on my neck she had licked were left to chill in the air. My mouth felt dry, my tongue stuck in places it shouldn't be sticking, and I swallowed. I hadn't said *it* before, that I loved her. It had been eluded to, she had guessed, but I had never *said* it.

I tried remembering the last time I said that I loved a woman—*Cheryl*—and I tried to pull forth in my memory just the way I left when I was with her. I couldn't, it had been too long ago, but what I did know was, it wasn't *this*. It couldn't have been, because that, I would have remembered. And then, I thought … How had I convinced myself that I loved that snooty, bossy, bitch of a woman, when it felt nothing like how I felt swimming in the crystal world within Snow's eyes? How had I thought I was deserving of something so boring and ordinary, when out there was this woman who could give me something that made me feel crazy, determined and proud?

She made me feel alive.

And she stared down at me, a single tear working its way down her porcelain cheek.

"Holy shit, Ryan."

"Yeah, I know. I'm sorry."

"You *really* love me."

"Yeah," I nodded, eyes closed, pinching the bridge of my nose. "Sorry."

She smacked my chest with both hands. "You idiot, why the hell are you sorry?"

"Because words are a crutch. I didn't mean to say it."

"Oh God, shut up. I was just saying that."

Opening my eyes, I looked at her, shaking my head. "I am so feckin' confused right now."

"Does it help if I say that I love you too?"

"Not at all. I'm still confused."

But I reached up with both hands, cupping her face. I pulled her down to me, kissing her with tongue and teeth like my feckin' life depended on it. Because y'know, it did. I finally saw our love for what it truly was. I finally had myself convinced that she was my reason for everything. For the past, all of my screw-ups, all of my disappointments—all of it.

She was my reason for living.

I did the best I could at pulling her pants out of the way, at shimmying out of my own, to consummate the affirmation of our love in the snow. The essence of who she was, dusting around us, catching to our eyelashes and matching black hair.

She smiled against my mouth, holding me inside her without moving. "I love you Ireland, and tomorrow, you're going to ruin my body forever."

And that was fine.

She had already ruined me forever.

CHAPTER FOURTEEN
ROOTS & FOREVER

She had been afraid of me.

Which wasn't all that much of a compliment, until she explained herself.

The last time anybody had said they loved her, they had only been using the words to get to her, to use her. She didn't want that to be the case for me, and then, I was flattered.

After she had left the douchebag, she had decided she was done living her life for someone else. So, she quit her job at the bank, and went into the process of learning how to tattoo professionally. She had already known the basics, from friends who were artists and getting work done on herself. Then she got an apprenticeship at a tattoo shop near her parents' place and hung out there for a couple years. Learning the ropes, perfecting her skills, getting licensed.

Her parents decided they wanted to move somewhere less humid but equally hot, and they headed out to Arizona, to be with the cacti and coyotes. Snow, however, decided she was ready to finally live up to her self-given name, and applied for some jobs up north.

The only one that called her back was Canvas & Ink.

"Well, shite, if anything could make me believe in fate …" I smiled at her back, as I ruined her body forever.

"Yeah, yeah. Ease up on that pressure there, pal. You're *tattooing* me, not carving a fucking turkey."

"Sorry," I grumbled, but I couldn't contain that smile, watching the needle jut in and out of her skin. Marking her for life. Ruining her forever. That soothing buzz, a lullaby into a place of serene euphoria at the process of doing what I had always wanted to do.

Christ, who knew I could feel that happy? Who knew I could feel so proud, and like I couldn't possibly disappoint anybody that mattered?

"How's it looking?" she asked, looking at me over her shoulder.

I wiped away the excess ink, the little droplets of blood, and sat back to admire my handiwork. The tendrilled lines. The sweeping black. "Ehm, pretty feckin' good, actually."

"Are you done yet?"

"Nah, ya gotta lie on the table."

"What? Why?"

"I gotta tattoo your arse, babe. Markin' ya for life."

"My *arse*?!" she mocked as she shot me a hard look over her shoulder, wide blue eyes both intrigued and terrified.

"Sorry, it's gotta happen. Why, you don't trust me?"

Her eyes softened, her lips smiled. "I'd trust you with my life."

"Good." I reached over her, patting the table's smooth surface. "Get up there."

"Oh, good Lord, fine. The cover-up I'm going to need is going to be ridiculous, I can already tell."

"Shut up and hop on." I laughed.

And then, she was naked, lying flat on the kitchen table, and I thanked Christ that Granny was incapable of climbing the stairs.

"I can't believe I ever agreed to letting you do this," she grumbled, her voice muffled by her arms, folded on the table. "When I told you I wanted you to tattoo me, I was thinking a little thing on my ankle or some shit."

I chuckled, working the needle over that delicious slope of milky white skin. "Hey, you can tattoo my arse too, if you want."

"Oh, I'm inking you all right, but it won't be your ass."

"Remember who's holdin' the machine right now."

She groaned, and then laughed. "You know, maybe I'll get something right above my crotch."

"Ehm, how above?"

"*Right* above."

"Well, if you do decide to do that, you're lettin' me do it. No way in feckin' hell would I be okay with some guy lookin' at my girlfriend's—"

She was laughing. "Oh my God, relax."

I grumbled, keeping my hand steady as I worked my way down. "What were ya thinkin'?"

"The Irish flag," she said, a giggle tacked onto the end. "Or maybe a shamrock. Or a pot of gold? Or, hey, what about a little Leprechaun? That'd be cute, right?"

I shook my head with a groan. "Next, you'll be askin' me to get matching ring tattoos."

I stopped the machine from moving, looking up toward the back of her head, watching for a reaction. My feckin' mouth; when had it gotten a mind of its own?

"Well, it's definitely something to think about," she said lightly.

"Not for a long time though, right?" I asked, prodding ever so lightly, testing those waters.

"Why? We're not bound by rules, remember? I mean, I did move in with you two weeks after we started seeing each other. That's a serious relationship no-no."

"Ah, right, and we did talk about our exes, and that's just …" I blew out a heavy sigh, shaking my head. "One of the worst."

"Exactly." I heard her smile, and I locked that bit of information away. About wedding ring tattoos.

Y'know, just in case.

৯৯

An hour and a half later, I had finished my very first, very large, tattoo on a human body. But not just any human body; the body of my girlfriend. The woman I was in love with, the woman in love with me.

I had been nervous. Terrified, even. But the moment that machine had started, and that hum floated into my ears, my psyche was thrummed into a meditation. My hand had remained steadier than I thought it would, the lines were mostly precise, and any mistakes that might have been made seemed fitting, in a way.

And this was the shite I thought about as I stood back, admiring my handiwork.

The first body ruined by me, forever.

The continuation of the tree on her back had been nothing but a series of lines, traveling down to the base of her spine, where it branched into tendrils of curling roots, cascading over her arse, stopping halfway down. Tedious work, and I couldn't believe she had let me after only a few weeks of practice. But there it was, now a part of her, and I wasn't disappointed. Not even in the slightest bit.

I took a picture on my phone and knelt at the head of the table. "Hey, babe," I said, nudging her gently awake. "You're done."

Her eyes blinked open. "Mm, I can't believe I fell asleep through that. God, I was so relaxed, even with you digging that thing into me."

"Yeah, I don't think I'll be diggin' anything into ya for a little while. You might not be sittin' down either." I held the phone out to her, and watched her eyes widen, as she took it in. "What do ya think?"

Her crystal eyes blinked, her mouth dropped open. "Oh my God, Ryan."

"You like it?"

She touched her fingers to her lips as she bit back the smile. "You did this *free-hand*?"

I shrugged. "Well, when you left, I filled a whole sketchbook and I hated it all. It was angry, and ugly, and I ripped them all out—"

"That explains the balls of paper all over the bedroom."

"Yeah, well ... After I knew where ya were, I went and drew the tree on your back. Or what I thought it should look like, and this is the basic gist of it."

She captured my eyes and held my gaze. "It's beautiful, Ireland. I think we found what you're supposed to do. How did it feel?"

I smiled, suddenly embarrassed. "It felt right."

"I'd say. We'll see how it heals; you might be going over some spots later. But I love it. So. Fucking. Much."

"I didn't ruin your body forever?"

"No," she said, tugging at my beard and pulling me in to kiss her, "you fixed it." And her eyes were fixated again on the picture, staring with awe and adoration.

That had been the idea, y'know. Giving her a base, giving her roots, giving her a home. Tying her down, making her mine. I wondered if she'd ever know that I had written my name in the mess of those roots. Subtly, among the gnarls and curls, but it was there. To mark her as mine … forever.

When her eyes finally looked up to mine, allowing me into that wintry world of ice and cozy warmth, I settled in, smiling. Mentally wrapping myself in the blanket I kept there, next to the fire I had built, embracing all of the chaotic unpredictability of being in love with her.

That was being with winter.

My kind of crazy.

EPILOGUE
ANNIVERSARIES & LOG CABINS

One year ago, Snow came to River Canyon. On the first day of winter.

One year ago, she waited for me outside the River Canyon Animal Clinic and asked me to have sex with her.

One year ago, I ignored the red flags, and went with it.

Christ, I'm glad I did.

I still worked at the animal clinic, trimming nails and making appointments by day. I was content. I liked the animals, I liked the stability. But then, at the end of my shift, I headed over to Canvas & Ink, where I apprenticed under the best tattoo artist in River Canyon.

If only I could stop staring at her arse long enough to get anything done …

I proposed to her one night after we closed-up shop. Tre had left early. He was doing that most days, since I started working there, and we had the place to ourselves. I hadn't really planned on "popping the question." It wasn't this big production or something I had spent hours of my time thinking over. It was spontaneous, spur of the moment, and just a little crazy.

"Hey babe, so our anniversary is in a couple weeks," I had said casually, wiping down my table.

Looking down at the shiny black vinyl, I thought briefly about the client that had just walked happily out of the shop: some guy from New London who had seen my work on the Canvas & Ink website. He had come by, asked for me by name, asked me to design a wicked looking piece to go on his shoulder, and that … Well, that was so, *so* far from disappointing. That was the shite dreams were made of. Something to be proud of.

Snow looked up from what she was doing at the autoclave and smirked at me. "I didn't know we even had an anniversary."

"Ah, of course. The first time you asked to fuck me, that's our anniversary."

She laughed. "Okay, sure, I can get on board with that. So, what crazy shit are we going to do to celebrate? Skydive over the Atlantic? Bungee jump off the Eiffel Tower?"

"Nah, I was thinking somethin' crazier than all of that," I said. I wiped my hands on a paper towel and said the very first thing that popped into my mind, just as she had taught me. "I think we should get married."

"What? On our anniversary?" she asked, and I nodded, tossing the paper towel into the garbage can. She quirked a brow. "You're serious?"

"Yeah, why not?"

"Because our anniversary is two weeks away. That's not much time to plan. I mean, I'd have to fly my parents out from Arizona, and then, we have all of your family from whatever Hobbit hole they crawled out of, and—"

"Da and the three of us are all over six feet tall, and my uncles and cousins aren't much shorter. Ya really think we came from Hobbit holes?"

She waved her hand dismissively. "You know what I'm saying. There's too many people to plan with such short notice."

I smirked, crossing my arms and raising a brow. "Do ya really want a big, fancy wedding?"

She didn't even hesitate. "Hell no."

"Sounds like there's not much to plan then." I smiled and walked toward her.

"God, you really want me to ruin you forever, huh?"

I laughed, wrapping my arms around her waist. "Babe, you've already ruined me forever."

Snow bit back her wide-spreading grin and reached a black-nailed hand up to tug at my beard, pulling me down to kiss her. "Okay, Ireland, I'll marry you. Let's do it."

And so, a week later, we flew Snow's parents out from the desert. I had been a nervous feckin' wreck, thinking about meeting them, but her mom—a little thing, just like her daughter—greeted me with a hug and an approving nod. Her dad shook my hand, treated me like a man to be respected.

Hell, he actually *thanked* me for taking such good care of his daughter.

Imagine that.

And this was the shite I thought about, while Mayor Connie Fischer, town officiant, prattled on and on about the sanctity of marriage. The importance of finding someone to spend your life with. There was something else, about respecting your town that made me narrow my eyes briefly, and I turned to glance at the crowd of people behind us.

Snow's parents smiled warmly beside my parents, who beamed with pride. There was Granny, thrilled that Snow was with us to stay, to invade her space and steal her tea. Patrick, my chosen witness; Kinsey, Snow's chosen witness; their two kids and her fresh baby belly, hopefully housing a boy for Paddy's sake. And lastly, Sean.

All of those people. None of them the slightest bit disappointed.

"Ireland," Snow hissed, pulling at my hand.

"Huh?" I turned back to her, a blank expression on my face.

Connie sighed with agitation. "Ryan, this is very serious business we're dealing with here. You'd be wise to pay attention. You wouldn't want to break one of your vows unwittingly, would you?" she scolded, glaring up at me through brows that looked maybe a little too thin.

My eyes widened with feigned terror. "Can't say I'd like to piss this one off, no."

"Then, for the love of God, listen," she snapped, and Snow bit down hard on her soft, pink lips.

"Ryan, repeat—" Connie tapped my shoulder, and I cleared my throat, straightened my back. She twisted her lips around her frustration. "Repeat. After. Me."

"You got it, Mayor."

"I, Ryan Seamus—"

"Your middle name is Seamus?" Snow interrupted, and Connie rolled her eyes, smacking her little book against her pudgy thigh.

"Yep," I said with a grin.

"Jesus, that's *really* Irish."

"She didn't know your middle name, Ryan?" Sean piped in with a little shake of his head, and I shot him a hard look.

"Can we *please* pay attention? I *am* missing the William Fuller lighting for this, you know." The

Mayor was tapping her toe, practically frothing at the mouth at the group of us, and I nodded as I mumbled, "If you think *that's* Irish, Sean's middle name is Fintan" through the side of my mouth, and Snow giggled.

"I, Ryan Seamus Kinney, take Ethel—"

I had been following along, reciting every word with great purpose, until my eyes damn near popped out of my head at the mention of the name I had never heard.

"Wait, wait, wait a second … Your name is *Ethel*?"

Snow only groaned.

"Focus!" Connie shouted. "I, Ryan Seamus Kinney, take Ethel Catherine Lewis to be my lawfully wedded wife …" I did as I was told, repeating dutifully, while thinking about her name.

Ethel Catherine Lewis. Christ almighty, that didn't fit her at all, did it? It was her birthname, but that was all. Nothing fit her nearly as much as that one word: *Snow*. She would never be anything less to me.

Snow. Winter.

Mine.

It was her turn, and I'll be honest, I didn't listen to a word she was saying when she vowed to take me as her husband. I was too busy, constructing my log cabin in the icy world in her eyes. A permanent home, a place to be proud of the man I had become. Granted, I wasn't much of a handyman, so it was likely to collapse come the next blizzard, but I'd weather the storm. We'd make it through.

She wasn't leaving, she wasn't going anywhere. I'd just climb back in, and I'd rebuild.

"—rings?"

"What?"

Snow sighed. "The *rings*, Ryan."

"Ah, right." I turned to Patrick, who dropped the two cheap placeholders into my hand. "Got 'em." I slid hers onto a slender finger, and then, there was mine. We turned to Connie with impatient excitement, and she waved her hands in the air.

"Okay, okay. I now pronounce you husband and wife. Go ahead and kiss your bride."

"Feck yes," I growled as I wrapped my arms around my wife, attacking her lips like I had been deprived, engulfing her mouth with my tongue, and she whimpered, going limp against me.

Snow's parents turned awkwardly to each other, grimacing a bit.

"Oh, Jesus," Patrick groaned. "Meghan, close your eyes."

"*God*, Daddy. You act like I don't watch TV."

"Yeah, well, you don't need to be seein' your uncle do the stuff ya see on TV."

"*Ryan*, that's enough now," Mam finally scolded.

It took my hand roaming down Snow's back for her to finally say something, and I was proud of her.

Our celebratory dinner was held at Mam and Da's place.

They had insisted on making us dinner—another dry roast and over-boiled potatoes. Snow's parents relaxed a little more in the comfort of the homely dining room, and they told stories about their daughter, growing up in a world I couldn't imagine her in.

Beaches and sun. Sand and ocean.

We weren't far from it all where we lived now, in that little coastal town in Connecticut, but we had the cold. We had the snow.

It was where she belonged.

"She absolutely *hated* the beach," her mother said with a forlorn sigh. "We always tried to get her to go, but she'd end up sitting under an umbrella, complaining the whole time."

"She never took the heat well," her father chuckled before taking a swill of beer.

"Her? At the beach?" Kinsey laughed, bumping her shoulder against Snow's. "Pictures or it didn't happen."

"Guys, I'm sitting *right here*," she said lightheartedly, sitting so close to me, I could feel her blood pumping through her veins.

Her mother waved a dismissive hand. "At least you found yourself a man who doesn't look like he'd step foot on a beach either," she teased gently as her wine glass met her lips.

I laughed, wrapping my arm tighter around Snow's shoulders. "Nah, I'm not much of a sun and sandals kind of guy."

"And this is why the two of them sleep in coffins, propped up against the wall," Patrick chided.

And I took the teasing. I smiled, and I laughed. But mostly, I stared at her. That strange feckin' woman, my *wife*, who I was still learning things about. But all of those things—her name, the things she did before she met me, her life of beaches and sun—none of them seemed to matter as much as one simple fact:

I loved her.

What else did I really need to know?

&❧

After returning home, after tattooing our matching Celtic-knotted wedding bands onto each other, after we had settled Snow's parents onto the spare bed in her studio, we went to bed with the disdain that we'd have to behave ourselves.

Or at the very least, stay quiet.

I helped unzip her dress in front of the mirror, watching the reflection as the straps drooped seductively over her inked arms. Revealing the black lace bra underneath, her two-times pierced navel, and then, her matching thong. Underneath that little strip of see-through material, I saw the glistening of silver between her legs, and I bit my lower lip. I caught her eyes in the mirror, satisfied with the sharp inhale through her nose when I pressed my erection into her back.

"Ireland," she warned, slowly shaking her head as the red dress pooled at her feet.

"We'll be quiet." I stood back, tracing the outline of the tree with the tips of my fingers, stroking the trunk along her spine, sliding under the waistband of her panties.

"You know we can't be quiet," she said, shooting me an icy glare in the mirror.

"First time for everything. And if ya can't, I'll have to put somethin' in your mouth, won't I?"

She turned around, looping her arms around my neck. "Well, I never do complain about *that* ..."

And just as I was about to lower my lips to hers, her eyes flitted to the side, and caught sight of something at the always-open window. Her smile started at her lips and traveled upward to crinkles the corners of her eyes.

"It's snowing?"

She nodded, toying gently with the hair at the back of my neck. "Yep."

We scrambled for our pants, her tank top, my sweatshirt, and I grabbed the blanket from the bed, and we hurried to the door and up the outdoor steps. I laid the blanket on the ground, dropped to my knees, and pulled her down to me. She found a comfortable spot against my chest, and I folded us up in our cocoon. Not to sprout our wings, to transform into more acceptable versions of ourselves, but to just be who we are. Wrapped up in the perfectly imperfect beauty of us.

"You made this happen," I laughed, looking up at the fluffy flakes, drifting from the sky and sticking to my lashes. "You just *had* to make it snow on our wedding night."

"I can't control the weather, you idiot."

"If you can control me, you can control anything."

"Yeah." She smiled against my chest. "That might be true. But you love it."

"I do," I said, threading my fingers into her hair. "I love *you*."

"I love you too, Ireland." And she sighed.

We laid there on the dead-brown grass, listening to the gentle hush of snowfall. The world was quiet, a sample of the silent Holy night heading our way in just a few days. I smiled, feeling content with my life. *Happy*. I was happy. I had been happy for an entire year, and I could only assume that my life would only get better.

"What are you thinkin'?"

"I'm thinking that we should open a joint bank account, and I'll handle the bills."

A thirty-one-year-old married man shouldn't be under his parents' consented control, and I laughed. "That's a good idea."

"I'm also thinking you should check your pocket."

"Or we could do something else instead," I said with a grin at the sky, reaching to grope her through the thin material of her tank top.

"I'm serious, Ryan," she whined, and rolled over to straddle me.

I looked up to her with confusion, gripping her waist in my hands. "This might be a problem. My pants are still on, and so are yours."

Then, she reached into my sweatshirt pocket and pulled something out. "Look at this first." With a smirk, she dropped it on my chest, and I released my hold on her to take a peek.

"What's thi—" I picked it up, knowing immediately what it was, and I sat up, pushing my chest against hers. My brows furrowed in deep concentration, holding the pregnancy test in my hand. I couldn't remember what the stupid box had said; two lines for positive, or was it one? I looked up to her for answers, and she rolled her eyes playfully.

"Really, Ireland? Would I be making a show of it if it weren't positive?"

"Get the hell out."

She pressed her hands to my cheeks, smiling with her icy, crystal eyes. "We reproduced, babe."

"Holy shite." I seemed to deflate with my exhale, but inhaling … My heart—my feckin' heart—couldn't possibly get any fuller. I gnawed at my lower lip, but it was a grin that couldn't be fought. I looked to her and said, "We're gonna screw that kid up."

"Nah," she said, tugging at my beard, pulling me toward her lips. "They're going to be fine. I mean, we are."

And I had to smile wider at that, had to pull her to me in the flurry, to consummate our marriage, knowing that any baby of ours would be perfect. Never a disappointment.

Our type of crazy.

Fine.

A NOTE FROM ME TO YOU

So, Dearie, what do you think? Is there a type of crazy for everybody?

Have you found yours?

I hope you enjoyed your stay with the "freaks" of River Canyon. The black-haired duo, thriving on the cold and chaos. I hope you were able to look beyond the tattoos and the metal, beyond the tough exterior, and into the unconventional mushiness of Ryan's thoughts.

I hope you're looking forward to your next trip into this little town, where everything means everything.

Until then, keep reading for an excerpt from Last Chance to Fall, Sean Kinney's story (coming May 2018) ...

LAST CHANCE
TO FALL

(COMING MAY 29, 2018)

It was five minutes to closing time when Jack the big spender stepped out of the elevator and walked onto my floor.

I sat at the computer, scruffy chin in hand as I scrolled through my phone. Just biding my time before the big hand landed on the six, and I heard the dinging of the elevator from just across the aisle.

Narrowing my eyes, I put the phone down to see a leggy blonde stepping out. She had a backpack slung over one shoulder, a braid cascading down one side of her chest, and she headed right toward me at the same speed as it took for my heart to stop.

In all of my thirty-one years of living, I don't think I had ever seen someone more jaw-droppingly gorgeous.

"I'm here to pick up for Jack," she said, her voice held tight.

"You're Jack?" I asked, untying my tongue. "Do you have I.D.?"

She blinked a few times, opened her mouth and closed it. She was searching for her explanation. I had seen the look too many times, after all those nights Ryan would wander in from being out all night.

"Yeah, I … Uh …" Her eyes closed, and she sighed. "No, I'm not Jack. *Jack* doesn't even know

I'm here. *God*," she groaned before looking at me again. "You know, I had this whole thing planned out before I got here, but I just can't do it."

I shifted uncomfortably in my chair. "Well, ehm … If you could just get permission from Jack to—"

The blonde shook her head, a few stray hairs falling against her ear. I had to resist the temptation to tuck them away, to brush my fingertips against her cheek, like a feckin' creep.

"Jack's my boyfriend. Well, actually, he's my *ex*-boyfriend. We just broke up yesterday. I caught him and his secretary, because *that's* not the most overdone cliché on the fucking planet, excuse my French. They were fucking in our bed, in our house, and so today, I did the most crazy I've ever done and shoved the fucking thing through the window and set it on fire. So, now I need a new mattress before I move to a new place, and—"

Her jaw dropped moments before she clapped her hands over her mouth. "Oh my God," she groaned, muffled behind her fingers. "I'm so sorry. I'm rambling, and I'm sounding crazy. I know you guys close in a couple minutes, and I'm sure you just want to go home and the last thing you want to do is hear the sob story from some crazy bitch who bought a ten-thousand-dollar mattress with her ex-boyfriend's stolen credit card."

It was taking my brain a few seconds too long to process everything she had said, but I had listened intently. Marveled by her glossy pink lips and the speed of the words passing between them. I finally exhaled, unaware that I had even been holding my breath, and I laid my hands flat on the counter as I slowly stood up.

"Listen," I began, finding myself out of breath from just listening to her. "Ya sound like you've had a terrible weekend, and I'd love to help you out, but if you're makin' the purchase without him knowin', I can't with a clear conscience allow the sale to go through. That's essentially stealing, and he could get you on fraud."

Her hands dropped and her arms hung limply at her sides. The excitable speed-talker had drained away, leaving behind this other woman, clearly broken and beaten without a bed to lay herself on. Her eyes glistened and she sniffed loudly, using her long fingers to wipe a tear away before it could even leave its watery trail along her cheekbone.

"I'm really sorry," I threw in for good measure, hating myself for being so careful with a book of rules to follow. For playing a part in her tears.

"No, it's not your fault," she said with a shaky voice. "I can't believe I pushed the fucking thing out the window and threw a match on it. I don't do shit like that, you know? I don't play with matches, like … *ever*. I mean, for crying out loud, I don't even burn candles! I use an electric wax burner, and it sits on a little plate on my kitchen counter without anything being—" Her lips stopped moving again, hung on the sentence, and she shook her head. "No, wait. It's not *my* kitchen counter anymore. It's *his*. Not even *ours—his*."

Her fingertips pressed against one temple, as though her head were all of a sudden killing her. Maybe she wished it would, with the heartbreak emanating from her like an aura. I could see it: glowing a moody shade of blue, haloing around her perfectly styled hair, encasing her slender body. She squeezed her eyes shut, pressing harder on the temple, and I knew I had to say something. I had to remedy the situation in the only way I could, and I dropped back into my chair, tapping along the screen.

"Okay, so you're gonna need a pretty big truck."

Her eyes snapped open. "What?"

"To transport the mattress," I clarified. "You'll need a truck. You ordered a California King, so it's big."

"W-what are you doing?" she stammered, blinking rapidly and playing with the end of her braid.

"Selling you a mattress." I looked up from the screen.

"B-but *why?*" Her voice trembled, her hands smoothing over the strap of her backpack.

"Because ..." And I had started the sentence with every intention of continuing it, but what explanation did I have? That I felt sorry for her? That I wanted to make sure she had a bed to sleep on? That I wanted to kill her boyfriend but couldn't, so this was the next best thing?

"You could get in trouble," she said quietly. She pulled her plump bottom lip between her teeth, biting gently. A line deepened between her brows. She was worried. "What if I just, um, put it on my own credit card?"

I looked up at her, arching a brow. "It's none of my business—none of it is, *really*—but can you even afford this? You know it's a ten-thousand-dollar mattress, and that's the sale price."

Closing her eyes again, she shook her head. "No, I really can't. Maybe, um … *Fuck*," she mumbled, fingers pressed to her temple, "why did I burn the fucking bed?"

"People do crazy things when their heart's been broken," I said gently. "My brother got his heart broken once and slept with a girl he feckin' hated." And why I told her that, I couldn't say. I scarcely talked to strangers, outside of customers, and I certainly didn't divulge the personal business of my family to someone I just met.

The blonde nodded, hands clenching around the backpack strap. "Hey, they say getting over someone is best when getting underneath someone else." She said it too matter-of-factly for it to be an implication of anything, but the words sent a lightning bolt of blood right to my groin.

After clearing my throat and licking my lips, I said, "That's all well and good, but he found out two months later that he had gotten her pregnant." Her brows raised with curiosity, and I shrugged. "He married the girl and was stuck for ten years."

"It happens sometimes," she nodded thoughtfully.

I smiled and replied, "Yeah, and sometimes people set their mattresses on fire."

To stay up to date on *Last Chance to Fall* (coming May 2018), as well as other releases, promotions, and exclusive content, follow me on:

Twitter: www.twitter.com/kelswritesstuff

Facebook: www.facebook.com/kelswritesstuff

Instagram: www.instagram.com/kelswritesstuff

Website: www.kelseykingsley.com

Newsletter: eepurl.com/c3K409

ACKNOWLEDGEMENTS

Let's see if I can get through this without forgetting anybody …

My family & friends: It always goes without saying that you will be listed first. You put up with my crap. All of those hours spent tuning you out for the sake of my imaginary friends. I'd like to say I'm sorry for that, but let's be real here … I'm not. But thank you for accepting it for what it is.

Danny: There's a lot to thank you for, mostly for being you and my type of unconventional. But right now, I want to thank you for this cover, because Jesus Christ, it is the embodiment of everything this book is, and you didn't even read it. Color me impressed! Thank you for that, and for everything else.

Jess: I am thankful for YouTube because it brought me you and this partnership we've developed. You are amazing and valuable beyond words. I love that you are my friend. I love that you love my books. I also love that you love that red pen, because you're really good at using it.

Jodi: I never like to single any one person out, because then I risk sounding like an ass for forgetting someone crucial, but right now … I'm singling you out. Because you, my friend, are a blessing. A miracle. A feckin' unicorn. Much of where I am right now, in this moment, is partially because of you, and I cannot thank you enough for that. Also, this blurb is incredible, and you've got that job until the world ends.

Jon McLaughlin: I'm thanking you for having the best music to write to, and for being cool on Twitter.

My Dear Readers, old and new: I love you most of all. Thank you for reading. Thank you for encouraging me. Thank you for randomly bombarding me with pictures of Matt Bomer.

ABOUT THE AUTHOR

Kelsey Kingsley lives in New York with her family and a cat named Ethel.

She believes that there is nothing better than a good doughnut and a cup of tea, and that there is a song for everything.

OTHER BOOKS FROM KELSEY KINGSLEY

Holly Freakin' Hughes
One Night to Fall (Kinney Brothers #1)

Made in United States
North Haven, CT
26 August 2022

23327888R00124